STOP!

This isn't a regular comic book!

In this comic book, you don't read straight through from first page to last. Instead, you'll begin at the beginning and soon be off on a quest where you choose which panel to read next. On your adventure, you will answer riddles, solve puzzles, encounter friends and foes, and collect magical objects—because YOU are the main character!

It's easy to get the hang of it once you see it in action. Turn the page for an example of how it works.

HOW TO PLAY COMIC QUESTS

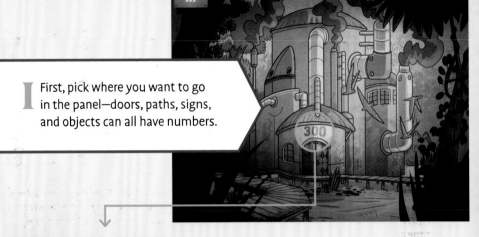

1 First, pick where you want to go in the panel—doors, paths, signs, and objects can all have numbers.

2 Flip to the panel with the matching number.

3 Continue reading from there, making more choices as you go to complete the quest.

HOW TO PLAY COMIC QUESTS

On your quest, use the handy Character Inventory and Spellbook sheets on the next pages to log your progress. Use a pencil so you can erase. (You can also use a notebook and pencil, or download extra sheets at comicquests.com.)

The rules are simple, technomage!

They will be explained as you play, but you can read them here as well.

YOUR MISSION: Your mission is complete once you have collected 30 points of magic energy and filled your battery. When you have the 30 points, go to panel 412 to finish your journey. Beware: Your quest may end early if you make bad choices and lose all your life points. If that happens, start the adventure again.

COMBAT: The Wheel of Destiny at the back of the book will determine the outcome of your battles. If you aren't using a borrowed copy of the book, you can cut out the wheel along the dotted line, lay it on a flat surface, and spin a crayon on it to determine your score. If you don't want to cut out the wheel, simply roll a six-sided die. Add the number you get to either your magic or technology score—your choice. This is your combat score. You have to spin once for yourself and once for your opponent. You and your opponent must fight with the same skill—either magic or technology. If the result is in your favor, you defeat the opponent. If the result is in your opponent's favor, you lose 1 life point and have to fight again.

MAP: There is a map of Paris after the Character Inventory and Spellbook pages. You may refer to it only when instructed to do so. Choose any destination on the map to go to, but first you must use the compass to navigate there.

COMPASS: The compass at the back of the book will help you navigate across Paris. You may refer to it only when instructed to do so. Either spin a crayon or toss a coin. Whatever number it lands on, go to that panel and see what you find. This represents your travels on the way to your destination. After that, you may go to the original destination you chose on the map.

PAY ATTENTION: Read the instructions in each panel carefully. Look at all the details in the pictures, for secrets are hidden everywhere. Keep your eyes peeled, and you may discover valuable items or shortcuts.

BE HONEST: Don't cheat! Do not look ahead to other panels and don't manipulate the Wheel of Destiny to win your battles.

GOOD LUCK!

Character Inventory

Magic

Technology

Charisma

Life

Accessories

Outfits

Weapons

Magic Battery

Items Found

As soon as you've found a piece of equipment (weapons, accessories, and outfits), write it down in the corresponding box around your character. You can have only one item in each of these categories at a time. Write down all the other items you find too. Keep track of your magic, technology, charisma, and life points. Remember to color in one segment of the magic battery for each energy point you acquire. Once all the segments are filled in, go to panel 412 to finish your quest.

Spellbook

You will collect different spells during your adventure. You may keep only two copies of the same spell at a time. As soon as you obtain a copy of a spell, check the box next to that spell, and then uncheck the box after you have used that spell. The spells in red can only be used during a fight, while the spells in green can only be used outside of a fight.

Illusion ☐☐
Swap your magic score with your technology score during this fight.

☐☐ **Shock**
Instantly defeat your enemy if their technology and magic scores are less than or equal to 10 when added together.

Evil Eye ☑☐
Your enemy loses 3 magic and technology points during this fight.

☐☐ **Vampirism**
If you win this fight, add 2 life points to your total.

Vitality ☐☐
Add 1 life point to your total.

☐☐ **Hypnosis**
Add 3 temporary points to your charisma score during this encounter.

Divination ☐☐
If you don't know the answer to a riddle, this spell allows you to proceed as though you have the right answer.

☐☐ **Alchemy**
Transform any item in your inventory into 100 francs. The object is then destroyed.

Character Inventory

Magic

Technology

Charisma

Life

Accessories

Outfits

Weapons

Magic Battery

Items Found

As soon as you've found a piece of equipment (weapons, accessories, and outfits), write it down in the corresponding box around your character. You can have only one item in each of these categories at a time. Write down all the other items you find too. Keep track of your magic, technology, charisma, and life points. Remember to color in one segment of the magic battery for each energy point you acquire. Once all the segments are filled in, go to panel 412 to finish your quest.

Spellbook

You will collect different spells during your adventure. You may keep only two copies of the same spell at a time. As soon as you obtain a copy of a spell, check the box next to that spell, and then uncheck the box after you have used that spell. The spells in red can only be used during a fight, while the spells in green can only be used outside of a fight.

Illusion ☐☐
Swap your magic score with your technology score during this fight.

☐☐ Shock
Instantly defeat your enemy if their technology and magic scores are less than or equal to 10 when added together.

Evil Eye ☐☐
Your enemy loses 3 magic and technology points during this fight.

☐☐ Vampirism
If you win this fight, add 2 life points to your total.

Vitality ☐☐
Add 1 life point to your total.

☐☐ Hypnosis
Add 3 temporary points to your charisma score during this encounter.

Divination ☐☐
If you don't know the answer to a riddle, this spell allows you to proceed as though you have the right answer.

☐☐ Alchemy
Transform any item in your inventory into 100 francs. The object is then destroyed.

Character Inventory

Magic

Technology

Charisma

Life

Accessories

Outfits

Weapons

Magic Battery

Items Found

As soon as you've found a piece of equipment (weapons, accessories, and outfits), write it down in the corresponding box around your character. You can have only one item in each of these categories at a time. Write down all the other items you find too. Keep track of your magic, technology, charisma, and life points. Remember to color in one segment of the magic battery for each energy point you acquire. Once all the segments are filled in, go to panel 412 to finish your quest.

Spellbook

You will collect different spells during your adventure. You may keep only two copies of the same spell at a time. As soon as you obtain a copy of a spell, check the box next to that spell, and then uncheck the box after you have used that spell. The spells in red can only be used during a fight, while the spells in green can only be used outside of a fight.

Illusion ☐☐
Swap your magic score with your technology score during this fight.

☐☐ Shock
Instantly defeat your enemy if their technology and magic scores are less than or equal to 10 when added together.

Evil Eye ☐☐
Your enemy loses 3 magic and technology points during this fight.

☐☐ Vampirism
If you win this fight, add 2 life points to your total.

Vitality ☐☐
Add 1 life point to your total.

☐☐ Hypnosis
Add 3 temporary points to your charisma score during this encounter.

Divination ☐☐
If you don't know the answer to a riddle, this spell allows you to proceed as though you have the right answer.

☐☐ Alchemy
Transform any item in your inventory into 100 francs. The object is then destroyed.

Map of Paris

This is your map of Paris. Remember, you may only use it when instructed. You may choose any destination on the map, but first use the compass at the back of the book to navigate there.

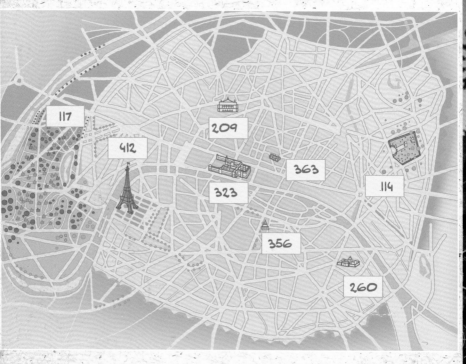

Map location numbers: 117, 209, 412, 363, 323, 114, 356, 260

Boulogne Swamp

Eiffel Tower

Opera House

Louvre Museum

Halles Mall

School of Technomagic

Père Lachaise Cemetery

Pitié-Salpêtrière Hospital

Paris, Spring 1889. Leaving behind the war and chaos of the 19th century, France enters a new era of peace and prosperity. The once-turbulent capital city is now the City of Light, from which culture shines across all of Europe.

At the same time, magic, once thought of as nothing more than a myth, has returned as the driving force of the Industrial Revolution. Magical energy crystals replace steam and coal to power machinery.

All these changes were born from the pain of defeat. On September 2, 1870, the French Empire was losing ground against the Prussian army. The French army was defeated by battalions of its enemy's artillery magicians. Faced with an alliance between magic and machines, France lost the first battle of the modern age.

The new Republic has worked hard to catch up. Nearly 20 years of peace and modernization have allowed France to return to the forefront of European culture. But the possibility of another magical attack on their soil haunts French citizens.

The World's Fair is the perfect opportunity for France to prove how strong it has become. In the heart of Paris, a gigantic steel tower designed by Gustave Eiffel is nearly complete. The Eiffel Tower will be presented to the world as the first counter-spell monument, designed to neutralize magic coming from abroad to harm the French capital.

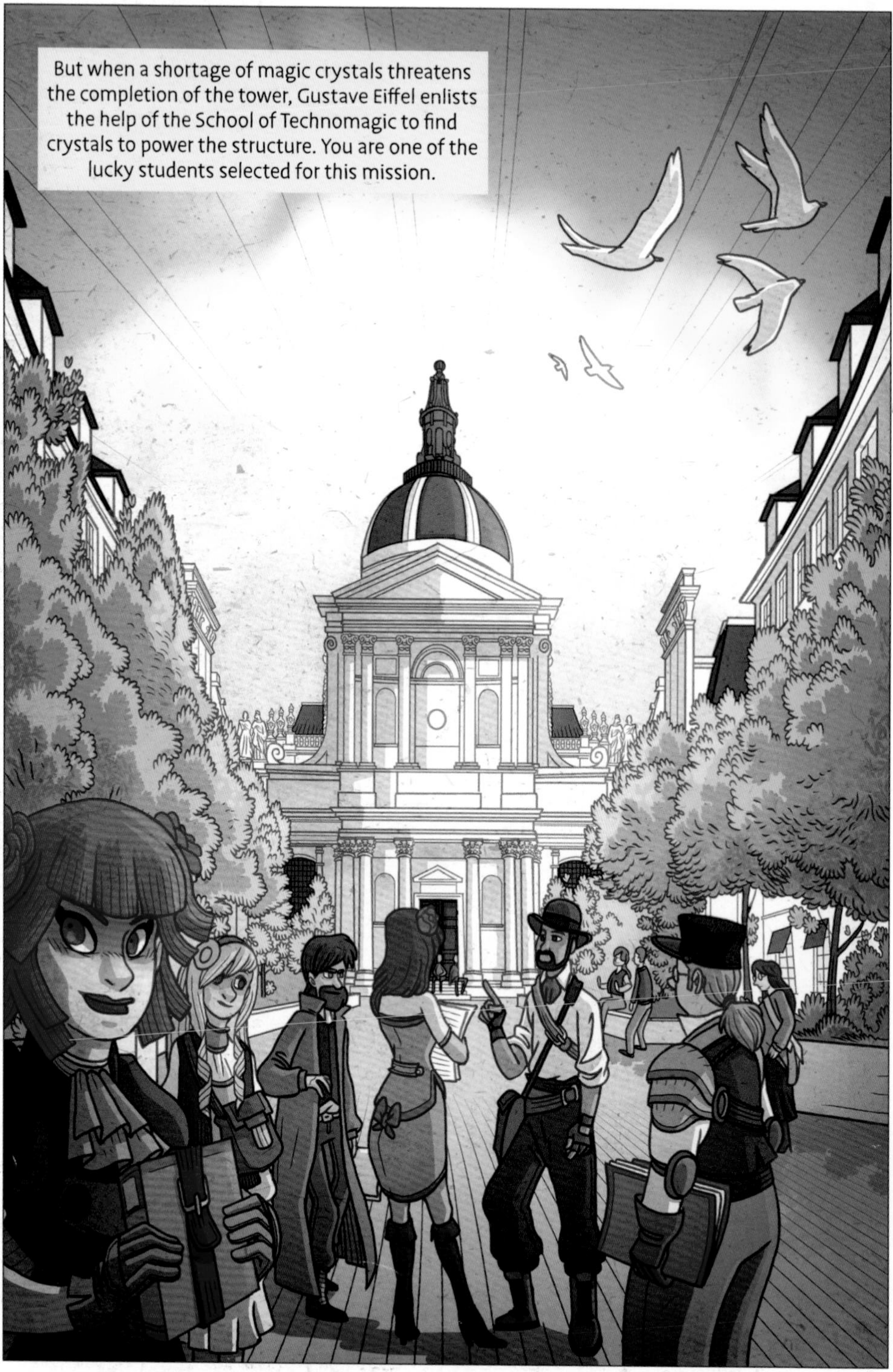
But when a shortage of magic crystals threatens the completion of the tower, Gustave Eiffel enlists the help of the School of Technomagic to find crystals to power the structure. You are one of the lucky students selected for this mission.

Technomagic is the art of blending new technological advances with ancient magical knowledge. Which character will you play?

BOY

Magic 7

Technology 3

Charisma 1

Life 5

GIRL

Magic 2

Technology 6

Charisma 4

Life 5

Once you have chosen your character, find their Inventory sheet and write down their magic, technology, charisma and life points in the corresponding bubbles. We'll explain all the rules at the beginning of your adventure. Now let's meet Gustave Eiffel on the next page.

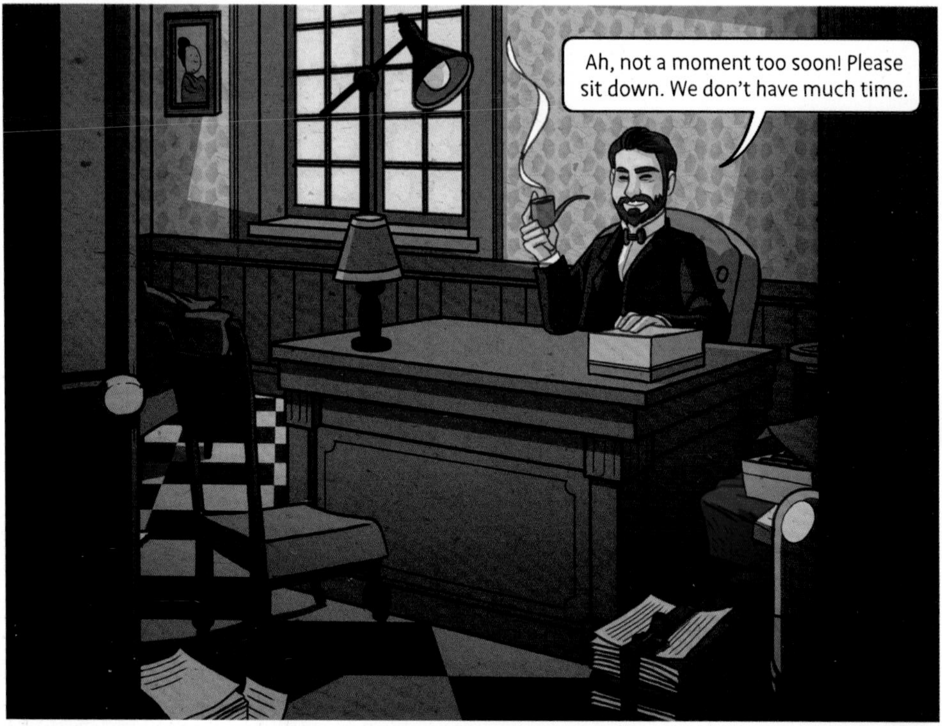
Ah, not a moment too soon! Please sit down. We don't have much time.

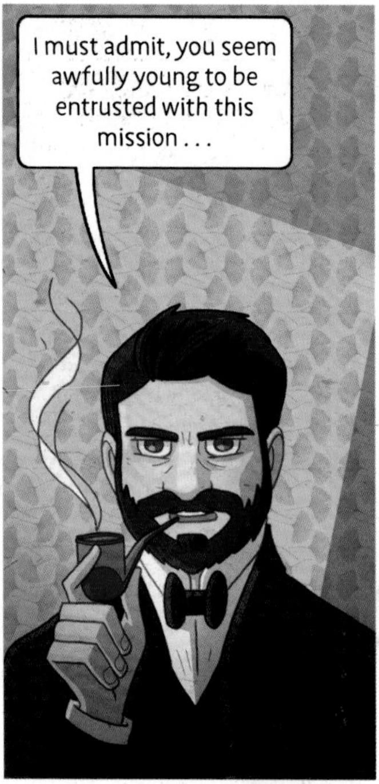
I must admit, you seem awfully young to be entrusted with this mission . . .

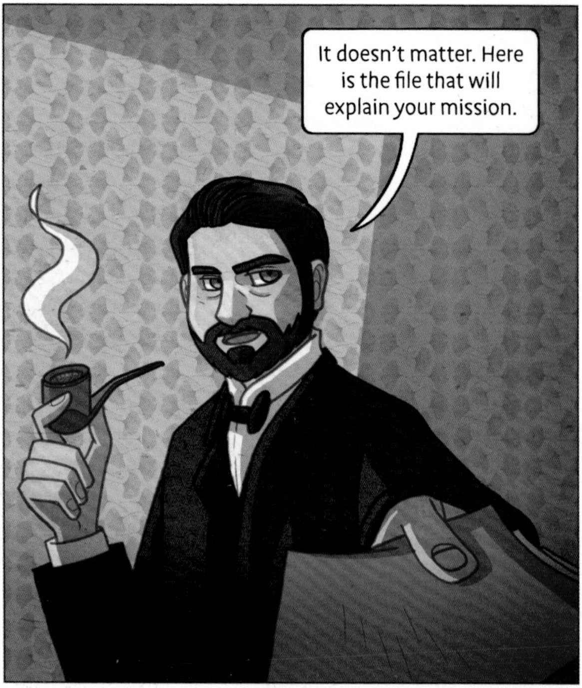
It doesn't matter. Here is the file that will explain your mission.

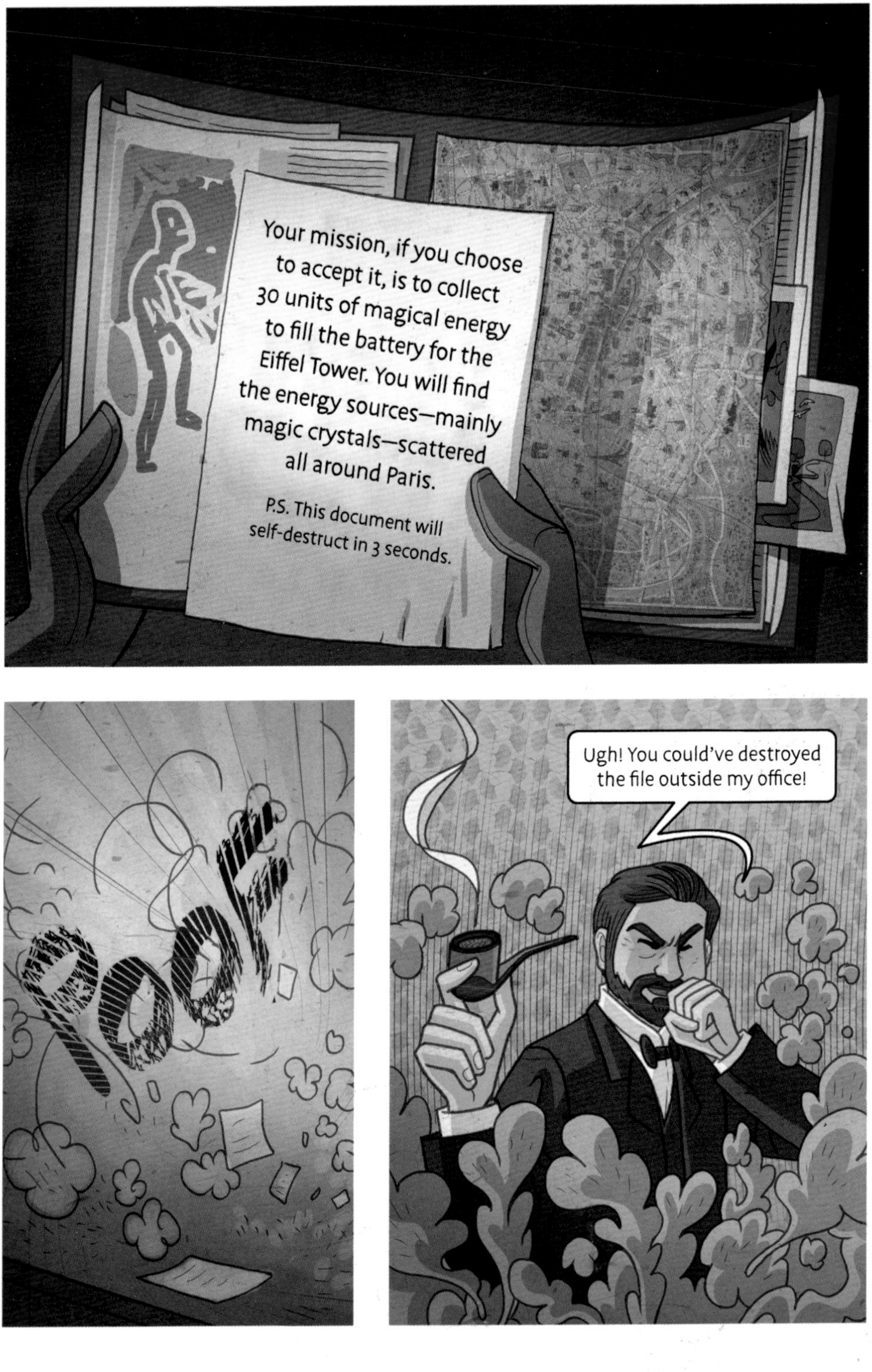
Your mission, if you choose to accept it, is to collect 30 units of magical energy to fill the battery for the Eiffel Tower. You will find the energy sources—mainly magic crystals—scattered all around Paris.
P.S. This document will self-destruct in 3 seconds.
Poof!
Ugh! You could've destroyed the file outside my office!

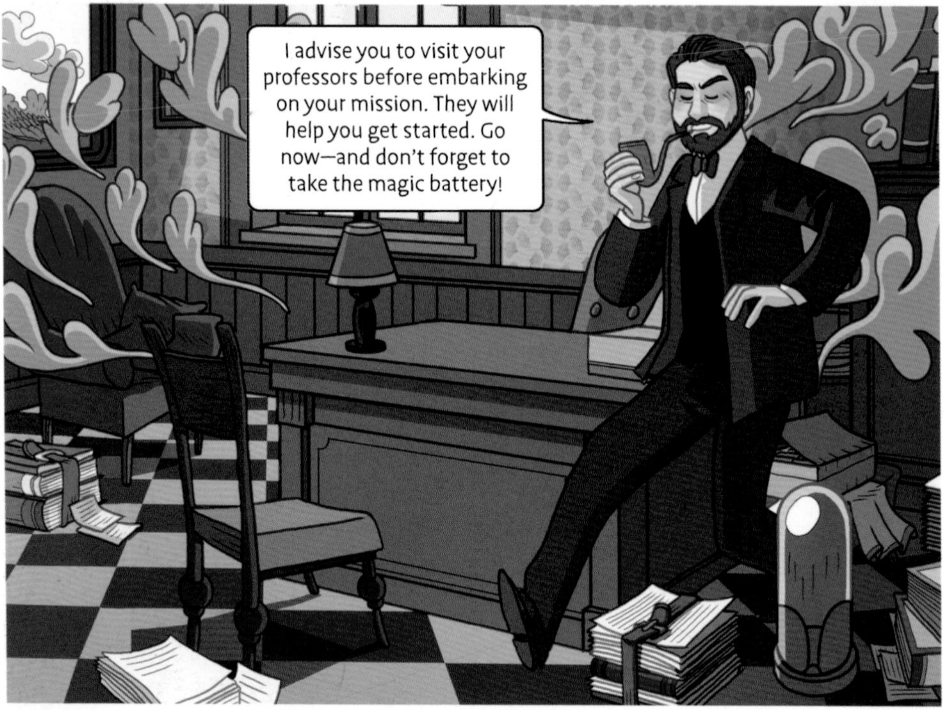
I advise you to visit your professors before embarking on your mission. They will help you get started. Go now—and don't forget to take the magic battery!

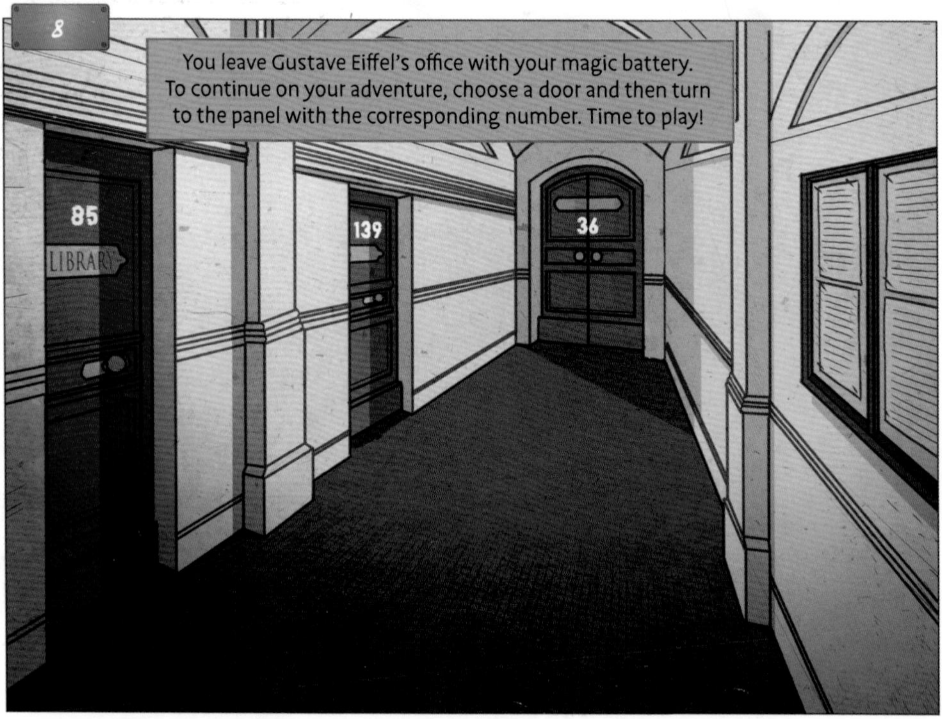
8
You leave Gustave Eiffel's office with your magic battery. To continue on your adventure, choose a door and then turn to the panel with the corresponding number. Time to play!
85
LIBRARY
139
36

The two possible answers are 75 + 12 + 9 and 46 + 17 + 33. If you found any other answer, you twist your ankle by climbing on a broken rung and lose 1 life point. Either way, you reach the platform in 61.

You're serious about this, huh? I'll let you in, but I'm not responsible if anything happens to you in there. Understood?

You listen to the gravedigger and decide to enter the gloomy cemetery anyway. Go to 104.

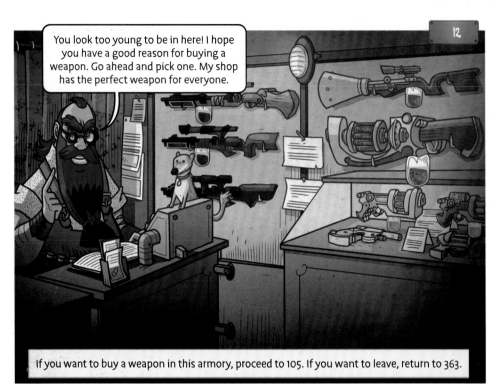

If you want to buy a weapon in this armory, proceed to 105. If you want to leave, return to 363.

Snow White won't let it go! If you've already come through here, you'll have to fight her again.

SNOW WHITE
Magic 4

Everything here is top secret. We're working to create combat beasts for the army, but they're not ready yet. What do you want?

If you want to see the secret project, head to 141. If you prefer to ask for better fighting abilities, head to 366.

Oh, I'm so disappointed . . . but your company did me good. I'm going home now. Goodbye. If you see my Ferdinand, tell him that I'm waiting for him.

You gave a little hope to the lonely ghost. Your charisma is now increased by 1 point permanantly, but you lose 1 life point. If losing 1 life point would result in your death, your life and charisma points remain the same. You solved the beggar's problem. Go back to see him in 193.

109

A ghost?! Maybe this is the shadow that the beggar was talking about. She doesn't seem dangerous. Be courageous and go meet her.

Uh-oh, you've come face to face with an animated skeleton! To attack it, go to 30. If you want to try to talk to it, head to 181.

322

370

117

CLACK

Click . . . click . . . ping! You cannot pick the lock or try again. Oh, well. Head back to 189. You won't be able to open this door, even with a weapon.

You think you're smarter than me, huh? You, a first-year student? We'll see about that! Here's the riddle I can't solve. If you can answer it, I'll give you a reward.

A father is 25 years old and a son is 27. How is that possible?

Try to figure out the answer and then head to 206.

At the end of a long and dark corridor you reach a room containing a sinister sarcophagus. Your hair stands on end as you realize that the sarcophagus is opening by itself! If you want to flee the crypt, head to 298. If you think you can take on the undead, go to 51.

Of course! I'm happy to help a colleague. My hands are full, so just take the keys off my belt. I'll see you at the warehouse.

Take the keys and head to the warehouse. Return to 64.

Someone is in this dressing room! Your interruption might annoy him, so if you want to leave quietly, head back to 285.

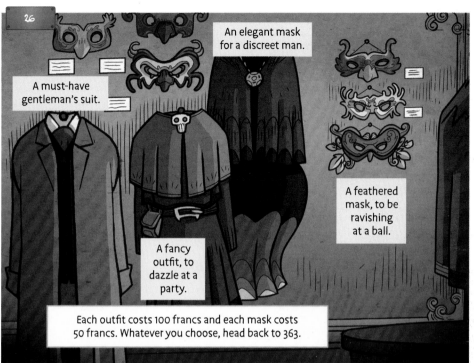

An elegant mask for a discreet man.

A must-have gentleman's suit.

A fancy outfit, to dazzle at a party.

A feathered mask, to be ravishing at a ball.

Each outfit costs 100 francs and each mask costs 50 francs. Whatever you choose, head back to 363.

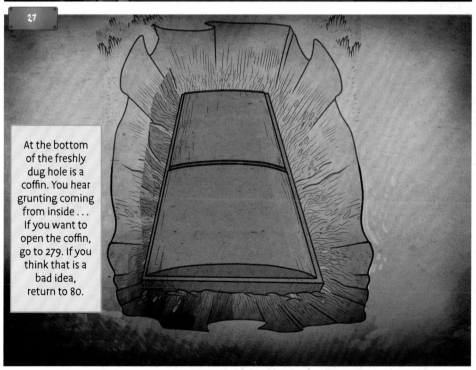

At the bottom of the freshly dug hole is a coffin. You hear grunting coming from inside . . . If you want to open the coffin, go to 279. If you think that is a bad idea, return to 80.

Congratulations! I knew you could beat that wild beast. If you are injured, I can heal you. During future combats, vanquishing an opponent can earn you a reward. I advise you to go to the library if you have not done so already. Good luck!

Your lesson is over. If you were injured by the combat dog, the professor heals you and gives back the lives you lost during the battle. Now head to 8.

I am so happy! It's so good to have you here with me again . . . Will you come back after work? I'll return to our house now.

You feel the coldness of death when you touch the ghost, but also the warmth of hope. Your white lie takes away 1 technology point, but adds 1 permanent magic point. You solved the beggar's problem, so head back to see him in 193.

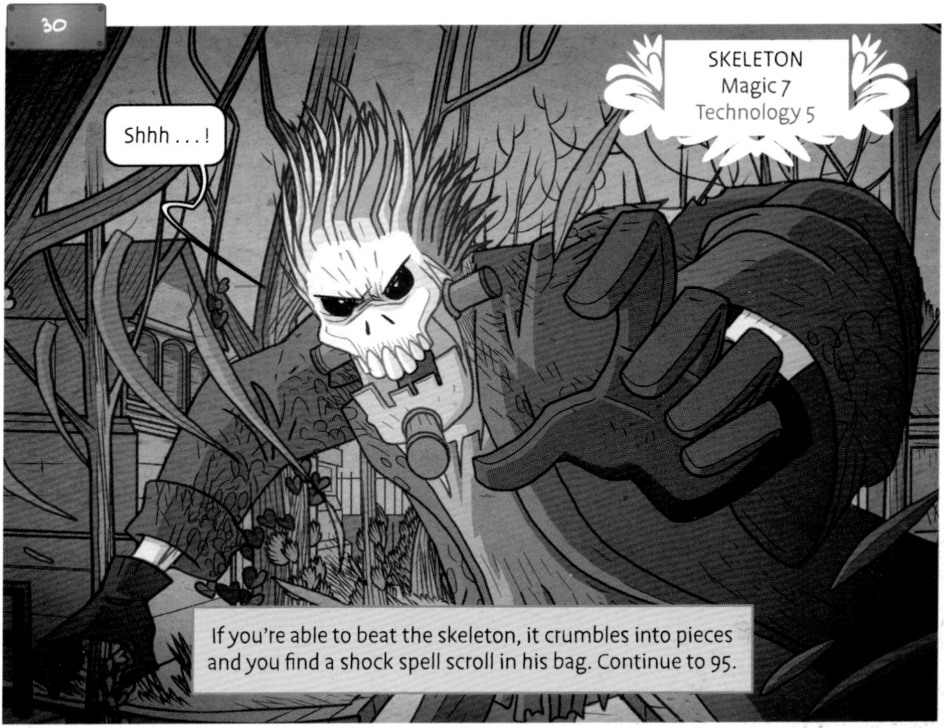
30
Shhh . . . !
SKELETON
Magic 7
Technology 5
If you're able to beat the skeleton, it crumbles into pieces and you find a shock spell scroll in his bag. Continue to 95.

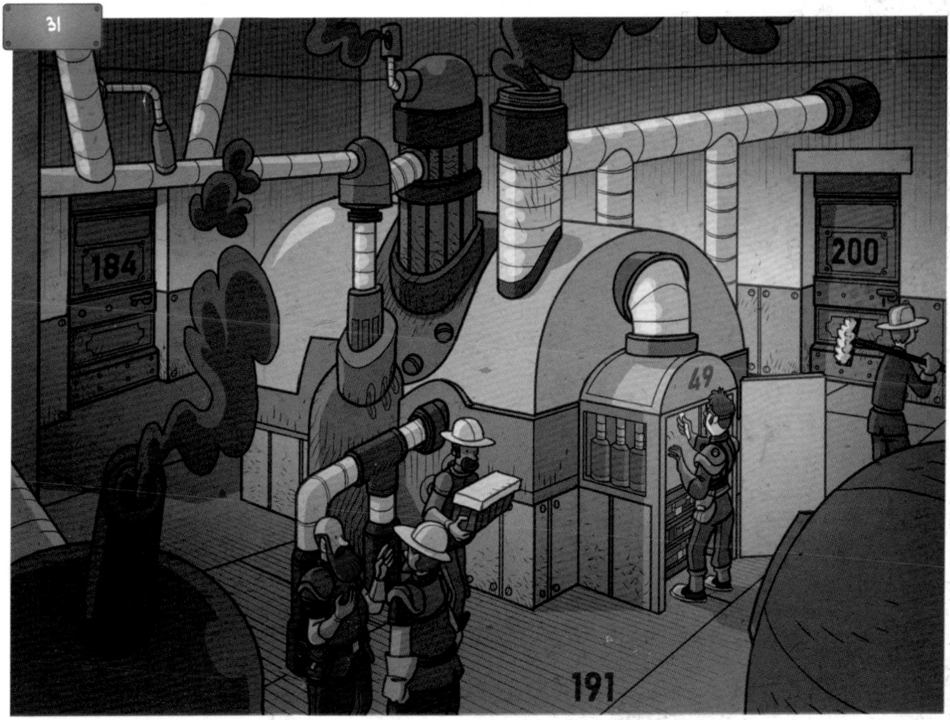
31
184
200
49
191

These pigs are really looking for a fight! If you've already come through here, you'll have to fight them again.

THE THREE LITTLE PIGS
Technology 3

Which way should you turn the first gear so that the piston makes contact?

I am sorry . . . as you know, one can never be too careful. Thanks for talking with me; our conversation changed my mind. I'll head back to the barracks now. Farewell!

The ghost gives you a shock spell. If you have more than 6 charisma points, he also gives you his red crystal, which is a magic source that adds 2 energy points to your magic battery. You solved the beggar's problem, so head back to see him in 193.

370

396

117

This is the door that will take you to the school's entrance hall. You can go through it in 182, or turn around and finish visiting the other rooms in the hallway in 8, which we highly recommend! If you do, you will learn a lot about spells and the rules of combat.

If you have 5 or more charisma points, you persuade the worker to lend you his keys to the warehouse. If your character is a boy, head to 24. If your character is a girl, go to 137. If you don't have enough charisma points, return to 64.

You find an old canvas bag with 50 francs inside. Interesting hiding spot! Head back to 165.

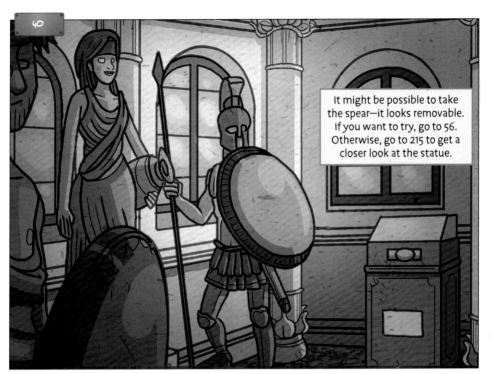

It might be possible to take the spear—it looks removable. If you want to try, go to 56. Otherwise, go to 215 to get a closer look at the statue.

I ... nom ... slurp ... am very happy to ... nom, nom, nom!

Okay, so bon appétit, I guess! Head back to 64.

This is the perfect opportunity to disguise yourself in his costume and head backstage. Up close, you'll be able to tell whether there's really a ghost that possesses the singer during the shows. Get dressed quickly and head to 212.

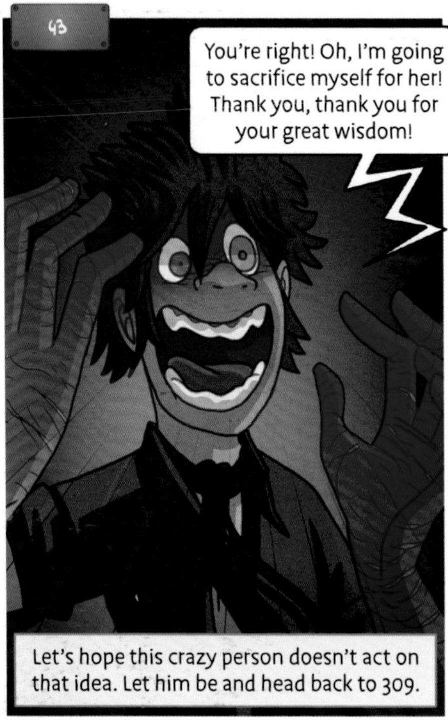
43
You're right! Oh, I'm going to sacrifice myself for her! Thank you, thank you for your great wisdom!
Let's hope this crazy person doesn't act on that idea. Let him be and head back to 309.

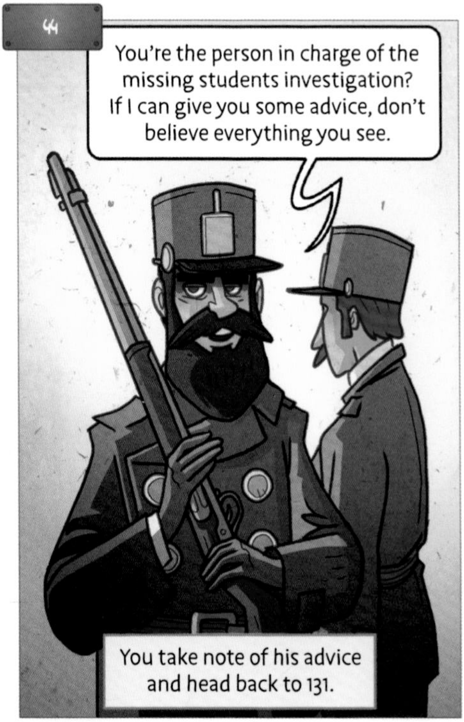
44
You're the person in charge of the missing students investigation? If I can give you some advice, don't believe everything you see.
You take note of his advice and head back to 131.

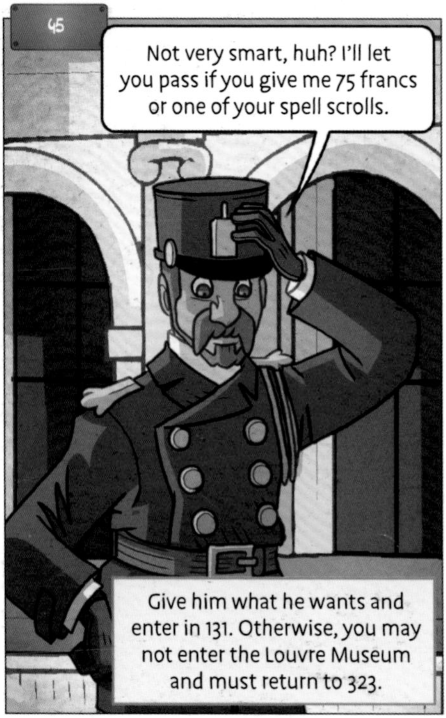
45
Not very smart, huh? I'll let you pass if you give me 75 francs or one of your spell scrolls.
Give him what he wants and enter in 131. Otherwise, you may not enter the Louvre Museum and must return to 323.

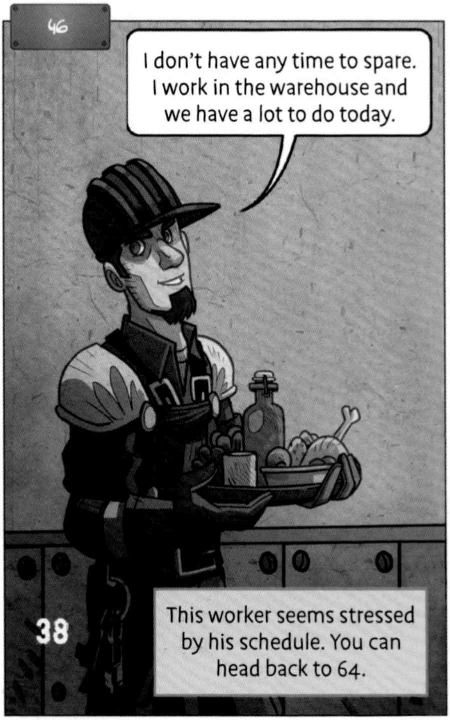
46
I don't have any time to spare. I work in the warehouse and we have a lot to do today.
This worker seems stressed by his schedule. You can head back to 64.

47

Have you heard the rumor? A ghost is possessing the singer at the opera house. My parents won't go there anymore.

Your folks are so gullible. I don't believe it for one second!

There's nothing interesting going on out here, but at least you've learned a rumor that might prove useful later in your adventure. You can head back to 182.

48

Thank you, thank you! You're a good person. I wonder if I can trust you because there's something on my mind that I want to share . . . .

If you have 4 or more charisma points, you can find out what this man wants in 58. If you don't have the points or don't want to listen, head back to 363.

49

Whew! I just can't figure out how this machine works! Could you help me?

If you want to help this worker, head to 33. Otherwise, return to 31.

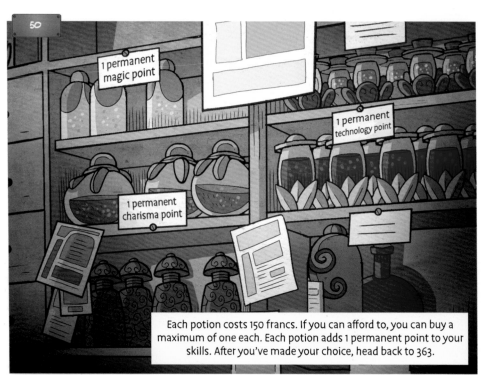

Each potion costs 150 francs. If you can afford to, you can buy a maximum of one each. Each potion adds 1 permanent point to your skills. After you've made your choice, head back to 363.

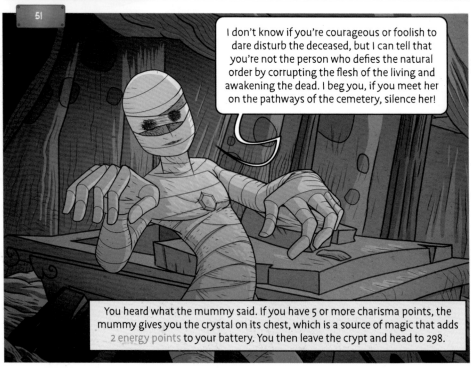

I don't know if you're courageous or foolish to dare disturb the deceased, but I can tell that you're not the person who defies the natural order by corrupting the flesh of the living and awakening the dead. I beg you, if you meet her on the pathways of the cemetery, silence her!

You heard what the mummy said. If you have 5 or more charisma points, the mummy gives you the crystal on its chest, which is a source of magic that adds 2 energy points to your battery. You then leave the crypt and head to 298.

50-51

52

The lock on this door is enchanted. If you want to enter, use any spell from your spellbook and head to 74. Otherwise, return to 64.

53

I'm sorry, but you can't enter the room right now. Please wait in the lobby.

Retrace your steps to 285.

54

Your keen sense of observation allowed you to spot the obelisk. You open the curio cabinet and take it. This is a magic source that adds 1 energy point to your battery. Head back to 131.

55

They're mine! They agreed to sign a pact with me because they are fools. But I will leave them alone if you sacrifice some of your life energy to me.

That doesn't seem like a great idea, does it? If you want to sign the pact in place of the students, sacrifice 1 life point and head to 410. If you refuse, or if that would kill you, go to 248.

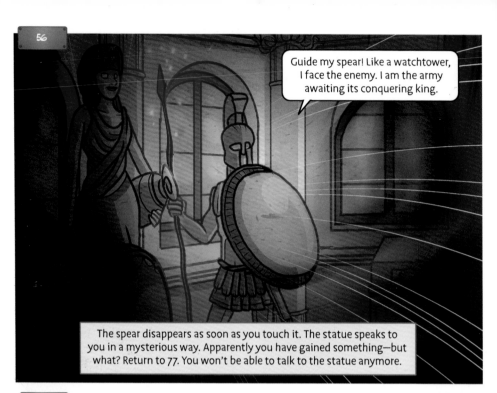

Guide my spear! Like a watchtower, I face the enemy. I am the army awaiting its conquering king.

The spear disappears as soon as you touch it. The statue speaks to you in a mysterious way. Apparently you have gained something—but what? Return to 77. You won't be able to talk to the statue anymore.

You'll have to decide which rungs to avoid before you climb up this damaged ladder. To figure that out, you must add up a combination of numbers that equals 96, using the fewest rungs possible. There are two possible answers. Each number can be used only once. Whether you figure it out or not, head to 10.

11
33
17
9
75
22
3
46
12

58

I saw some strange shadows around here last night . . . I don't feel safe. Would you mind checking it out?

Seems like there's something weird going on around here. You agree to help, and venture deeper into the city. Head to 98.

59

What do you want? Unless you know the password, you can't come in!

A female voice tells you to say the correct password if you want to enter. If you know it, head to 332. Otherwise, go back to 112.

60

Inside the box, you find a vitality spell and about 100 francs in coins. Please proceed to the Egyptian statue in 210.

The Daily Parisian

Zombies in Père Lachaise Cemetery!

The cemetery of Père Lachaise has been closed for two weeks due to incidents involving walking cadavers. The police investigation seems to be at a dead end. If you have any information about these events, please contact the nearest police station.

Doctor Charcot's Guests

Since January, the medical school has been hosting visiting wizards from Algeria. The group is led by Doctor Jean-Martin Charcot, who specializes in hypnosis.

Today's newspaper seems to have a lot of valuable information. Return to 182.

A dirty feral cat bites you! Because of your carelessness, you lose 1 life point. When you're done here, move on to 189.

To finish the mission, you need to completely fill the magic battery and then report to the Champ de Mars, which is marked on the map I just gave you. That is where the Eiffel Tower will stand during the World's Fair. I'm counting on you to complete your mission in time. Good luck!

This is where the tutorial ends. Please read the rules at the beginning of the book if you need more explanation. Now you can pick any destination on the map of Paris and travel there with the help of your compass.

You find yourself stuck in traffic, which is pretty common in Paris. Just wait a bit and the flow of vehicles will continue and you can be on your way. Consult your map to go to the destination you chose initially, or head to 207.

69

You find a weird figurine of a king in the nightstand. Take it and head back to 382.

70

What a pain! She refuses to let me in! I'm her biggest admirer! She's asking for a password . . . I have no idea what it is.

This girl won't be allowed to see the singer, who only allows those with the password the honor of meeting her before the show. Head back to 112.

71

Oh, yes! Ten tickles . . . like tentacles! Ha ha ha!

Ha ha! Let the student pass.

You've gained access to the Louvre in 131. Now you can find out what happened to the missing technomagic students.

Who is it? Why, it's the most promising student in school! I'm happy to have you as a pupil. I will teach you everything you need to know about spells. How does that sound?

If you want to know more about spells, head to 146. Otherwise, return to 85.

What nerve! I've never seen a journalist dare come in here. You can ask me one question, and then you must leave.

He thinks you're a journalist, so take advantage of that! If you want to ask him a question about the opera ghost, go to 138. If you prefer to ask him why he's so goofy, go to 118.

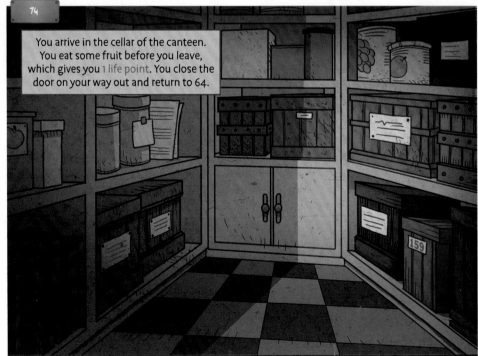

You arrive in the cellar of the canteen. You eat some fruit before you leave, which gives you 1 life point. You close the door on your way out and return to 64.

I don't get it . . . that was a bad answer.

This guy has no sense of humor! Anyway, you can try to convince the officer to let you pass in 45.

You find a small figurine of a farmer in the nightstand, as well as 50 francs. Take it all and head back to 178.

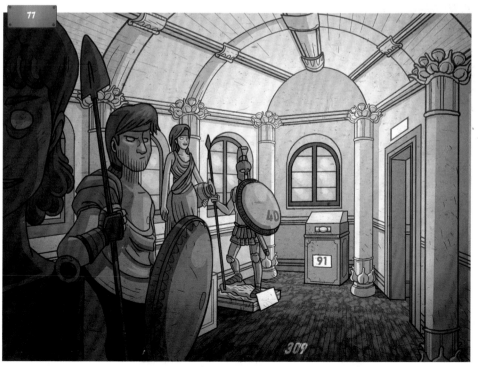

What a mess! If you're trying to make a good impression in high society in those rags, forget about it! Luckily, I have what you need. Make your choice!

If you want to look at the clothes in the shop and maybe buy something, head to 26. Otherwise, exit and return to 363.

What do you want? It's forbidden to enter the cemetery. It's full of zombies. This is no place for students!

If you have 6 or more charisma points and want to try to convince him to let you in, head to 11. If you want to bribe him with 100 francs, head to 86. Otherwise, it will be impossible to enter. Look at your map of Paris and pick a new destination, using the compass to navigate. You can come back to the cemetery later.

Do I know you? I didn't know you were performing tonight. Be quiet backstage, and be careful, too—the ghost must be close by, waiting for the opera singer! Kind of spooky, isn't it?

You won't get much more out of this guy, so head back to 165.

85

86

I guess we could all use a little something extra! Go on in, but if anything weird happens in there, you don't know me.

Sometimes you just have to pay someone off to get what you need. Enter the dismal cemetery of Père Lachaise in 104.

87

No! You're trying to trick me with your lies! AHHHH!

This guy is definitely crazy. He doesn't want any help and ignores you completely. Head back to 309.

I am the conqueror—pure and noble. I am looking for the weapon that will strike from a distance. If you can correct this mistake, the curse will be lifted.

This girl is talking nonsense. Head back to 382.

Ferdinand? Is that you, my love? I've been waiting for so long . . . Come to me!

If you want to pretend that you are Ferdinand, go to 29. If you want to tell the ghost the truth, go to 16.

You find a hairpin at the bottom of the trash, which will help you with a difficult door lock. You will be able to use it only once. Continue to 189.

The showcase window isn't locked. Your attention is caught by a beautiful golden ring. Whether you take the ring or not, return to 77. You can return here later if you wish.

What's the password?

The password was in the director's office in the form of a riddle: T4C. If you had the right answer, head to 103. If you didn't, go back to 184. You will not be able to go through this door.

Click . . . click . . . ping! You're unable to pick this lock and cannot try again. Oh, well. Head back to 189. You can't open this door, even with a weapon.

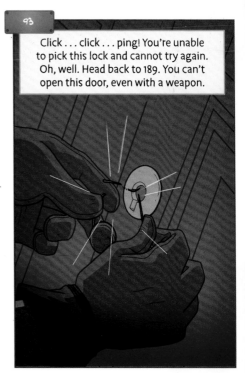

I always knew you were a quick learner! Now you know everything you need to know about spells. Take this spell. It will be useful on your adventure.

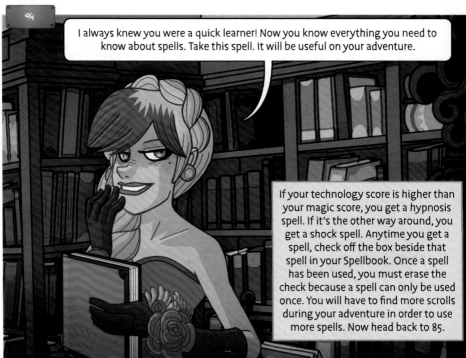

If your technology score is higher than your magic score, you get a hypnosis spell. If it's the other way around, you get a shock spell. Anytime you get a spell, check off the box beside that spell in your Spellbook. Once a spell has been used, you must erase the check because a spell can only be used once. You will have to find more scrolls during your adventure in order to use more spells. Now head back to 85.

This poor guy couldn't find his way out of the swamps. Now you know what's waiting for you if you get lost in here. Return to 9.

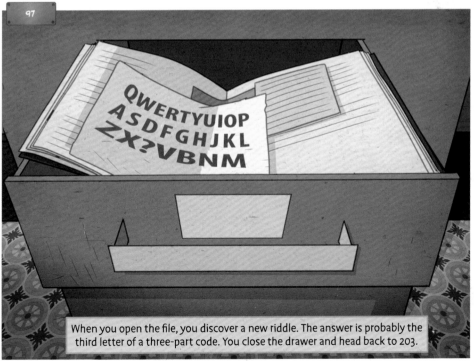

When you open the file, you discover a new riddle. The answer is probably the third letter of a three-part code. You close the drawer and head back to 203.

Annoying swamps! I have to cross this quagmire every day to work at the factory. I always need to rest afterward. Watch out—it's a real maze!

After listening to this man's warning, head back to 117.

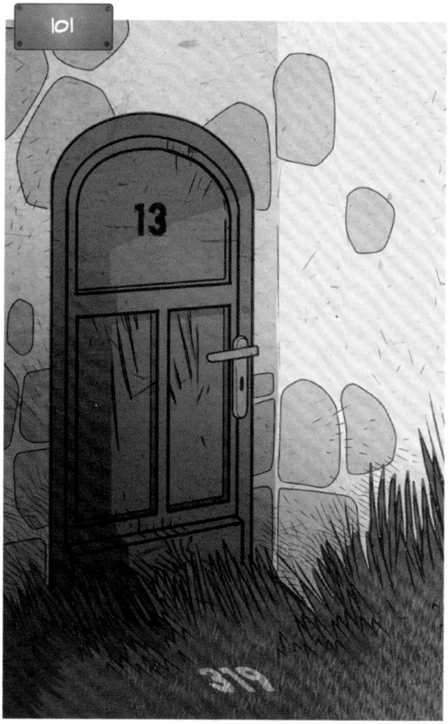
101
13
319

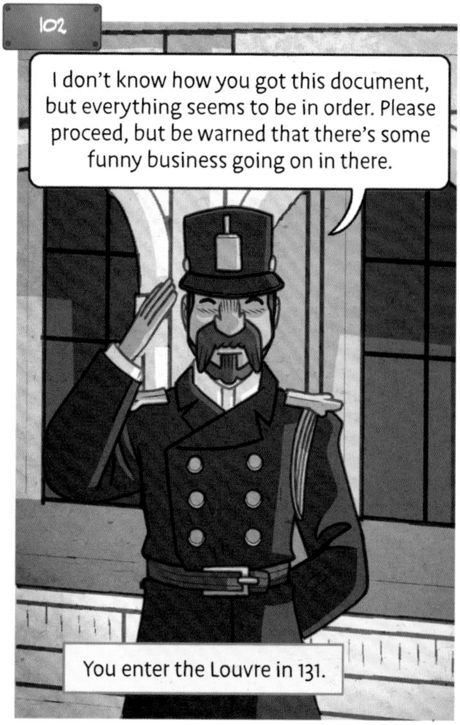
102
I don't know how you got this document, but everything seems to be in order. Please proceed, but be warned that there's some funny business going on in there.
You enter the Louvre in 131.

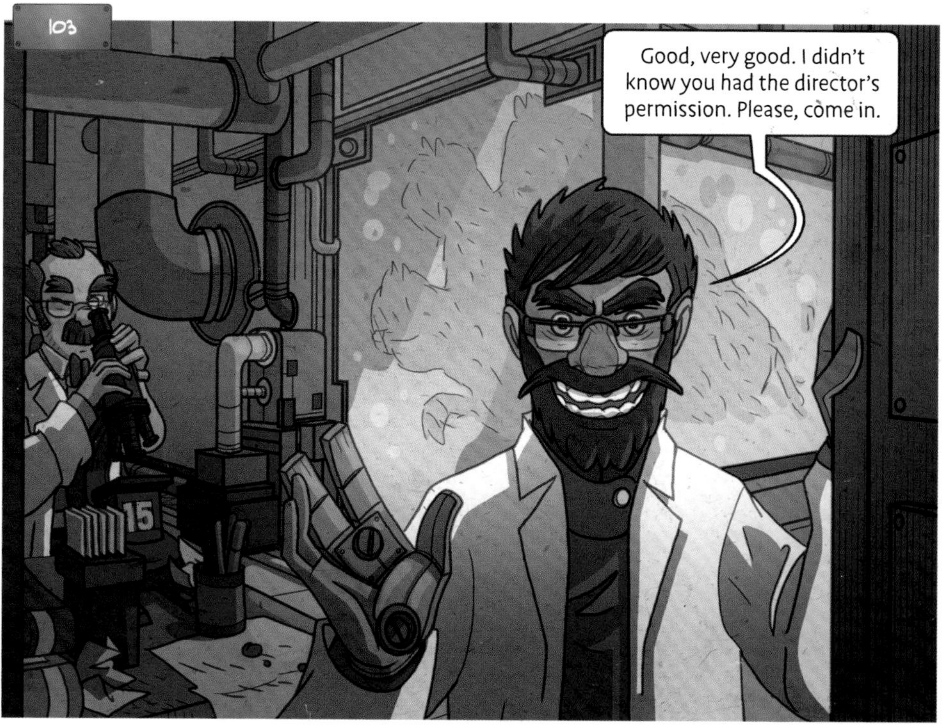
103
Good, very good. I didn't know you had the director's permission. Please, come in.
15

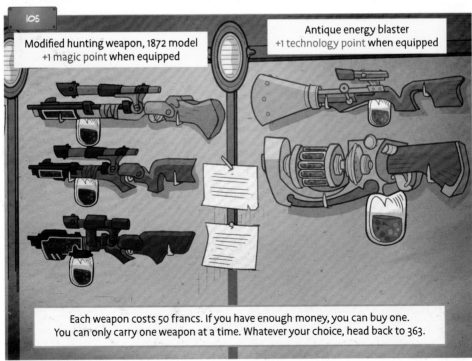

Modified hunting weapon, 1872 model
+1 magic point when equipped

Antique energy blaster
+1 technology point when equipped

Each weapon costs 50 francs. If you have enough money, you can buy one.
You can only carry one weapon at a time. Whatever your choice, head back to 363.

106

In the nightstand, you find a strange figurine of an archer. Take it and head back to 221.

107

32 283

174

108

Oh, yes . . . very good! Thank you. Here, take this—I don't know what it's good for.

The grateful worker gives you a shock spell. Head back to 31.

109

Who's there? I can't really see you, it's so dark . . .

If your character is a boy, go to 89.
If your character is a girl, go to 133.

110

TYPHOID MARY
Magic 8
Technology 4

HENCHMAN
Magic 4
Technology 4

HENCHMAN
Magic 4
Technology 4

HENCHMAN
Magic 4
Technology 4

During this fight, Typhoid Mary spits poisonous gas at you, which causes your magic and technology scores to drop by 1 point each. You also have to beat the three henchmen behind her. If you manage to defeat them all, head to 125.

111

GHOST SOLDIER
Magic 6

Once you defeat the ghost, the red crystal he held disappears into smoke. You gain 5 life points, but you lose either 1 magic point or 1 technology point permanently. You decide which. You solved the beggar's problem, so head back to see him in 193.

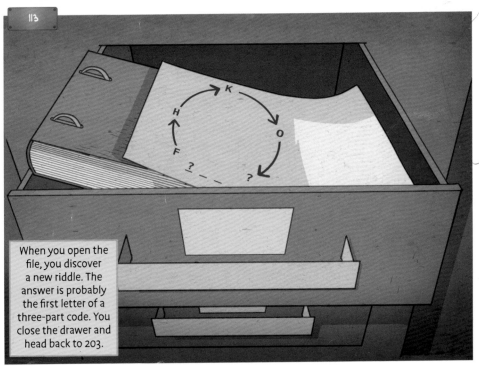

When you open the file, you discover a new riddle. The answer is probably the first letter of a three-part code. You close the drawer and head back to 203.

You arrive at the Père Lachaise Cemetery.

From here, you can look at the map of Paris and go to a different location, using the compass to navigate across the city. Otherwise, feel free to visit the cemetery.

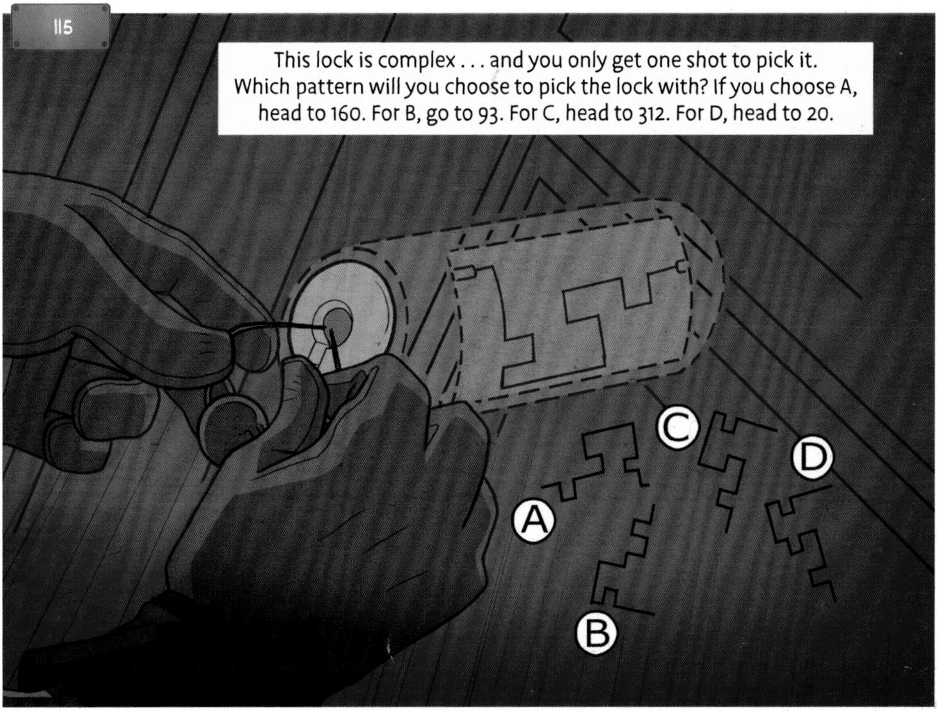
115
This lock is complex . . . and you only get one shot to pick it.
Which pattern will you choose to pick the lock with? If you choose A, head to 160. For B, go to 93. For C, head to 312. For D, head to 20.
A
B
C
D

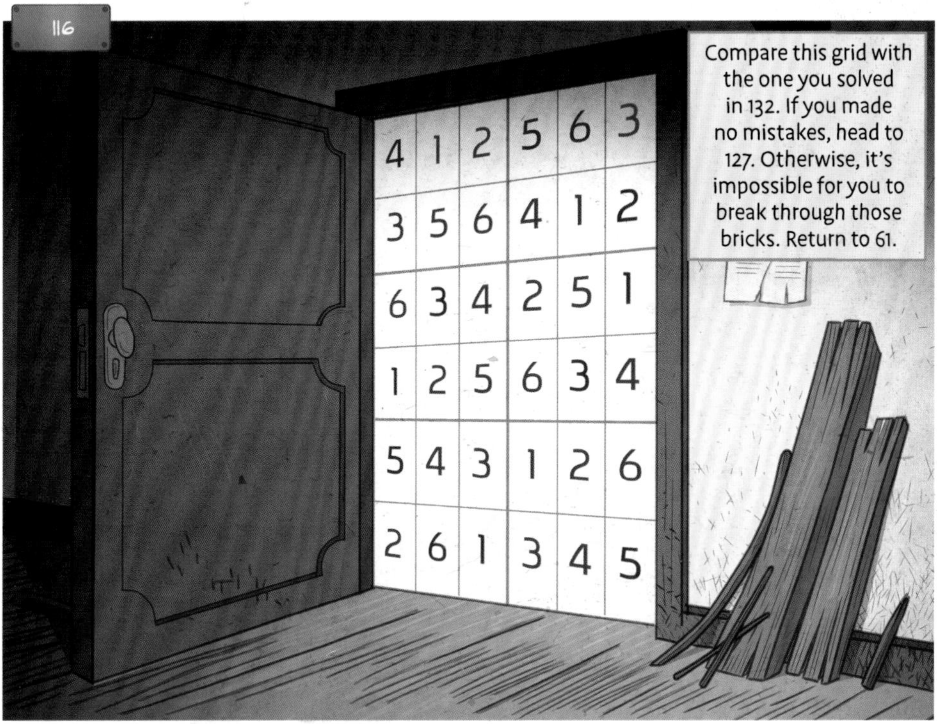
116
Compare this grid with the one you solved in 132. If you made no mistakes, head to 127. Otherwise, it's impossible for you to break through those bricks. Return to 61.
4 1 2 5 6 3
3 5 6 4 1 2
6 3 4 2 5 1
1 2 5 6 3 4
5 4 3 1 2 6
2 6 1 3 4 5

You arrive at the Boulogne Swamp.

From here, you can look at the map of Paris and go to any other destination. Don't forget to use the compass to navigate across the city. Otherwise, feel free to visit the swamp.

No one calls me goofy!

OPERA SINGER
Magic 8
Technology 6

That wasn't very smart (or kind). If you can neutralize him, go to 42.

Not bad, not bad . . . I guess there's still hope for the youth! As promised, I'll let you into the museum to look for your missing technomage friends. Good luck!

You enter the Louvre Museum in 131.

121

Very well . . . I know the secrets of your karma. It is time for you to enter the lady's sanctuary.

219

The doors open as soon as the voice falls silent. Remember your karma points—you will need them later.

122

You find a purple potion which, if drunk, will add 1 technology point to your score but remove 1 magic point from your score. If you decide not to drink it, it will stay here. You don't have any more time to look through the room. The show is starting soon. Go to 61.

123

"WHAT MAKES AND WILL ALWAYS MAKE THIS WORLD A VALLEY OF TEARS IS THE INSATIABLE GREED AND INVINCIBLE PRIDE OF MEN."
—VOLTAIRE

"FEAR THE DECEPTIVE ATTRACTION OF LIES, THE INTOXICATING SMELL OF PRIDE."
—JEAN-JACQUES ROUSSEAU

258

270

124

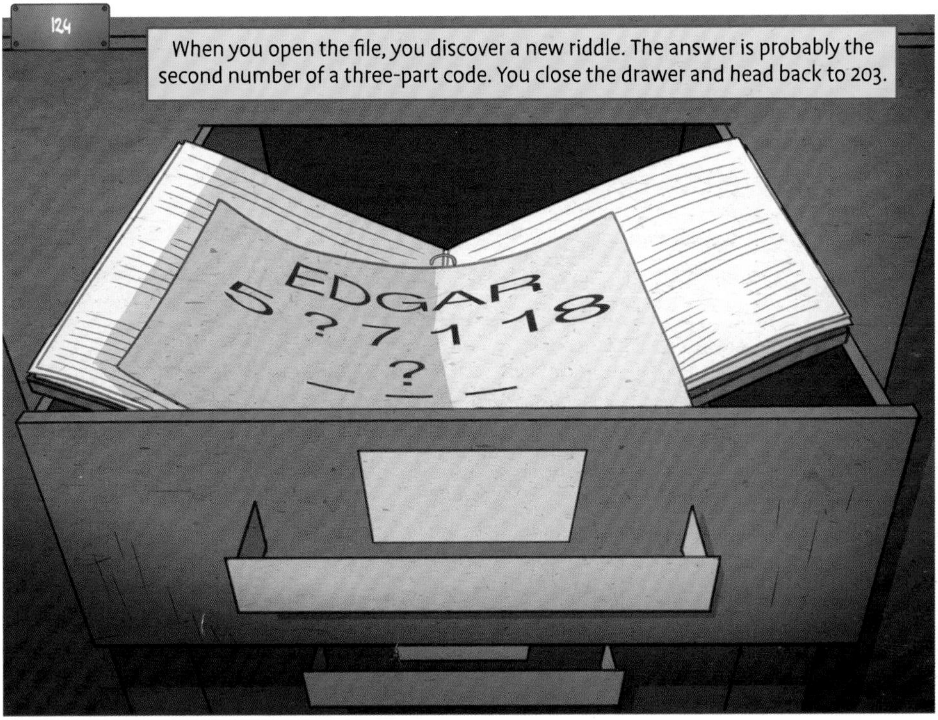
When you open the file, you discover a new riddle. The answer is probably the second number of a three-part code. You close the drawer and head back to 203.
EDGAR
5 ? 7 1 1 8
?
_ _ _

125

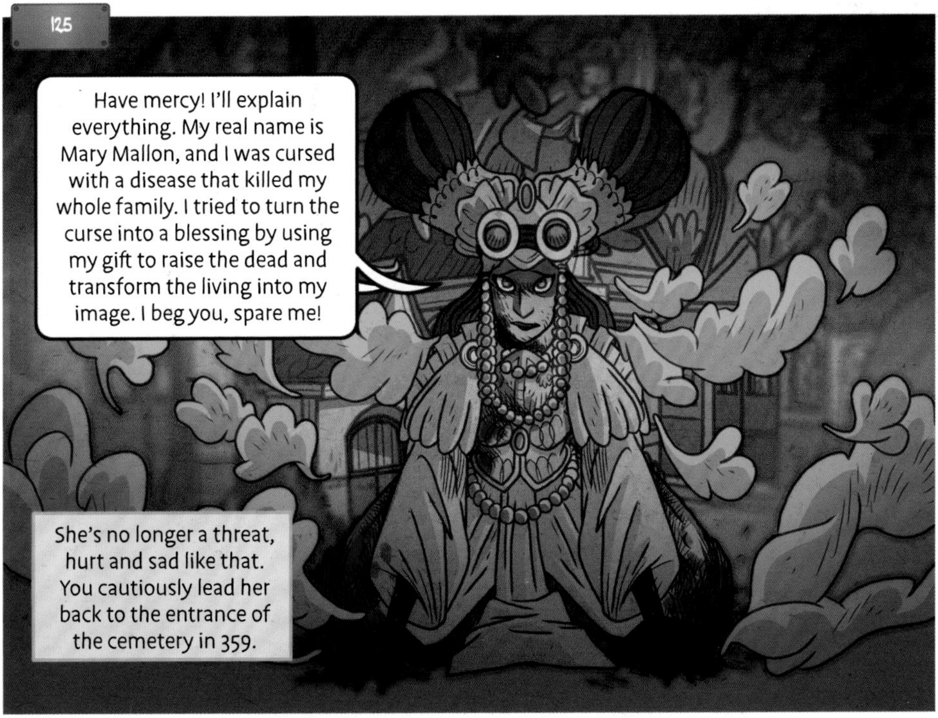
Have mercy! I'll explain everything. My real name is Mary Mallon, and I was cursed with a disease that killed my whole family. I tried to turn the curse into a blessing by using my gift to raise the dead and transform the living into my image. I beg you, spare me!
She's no longer a threat, hurt and sad like that. You cautiously lead her back to the entrance of the cemetery in 359.

126

Will you leave me alone? I'm having trouble with this chapter.

You bothered this student while he was studying. If you want to try to help him, go to 21 if your character is a boy, or to 225 if your character is a girl. Otherwise, go back to 85.

127

After you break through the bricks, you discover a coffin leaning against the wall of a small room. If your magic score is higher than your technology score, head to 339. Otherwise, go to 354.

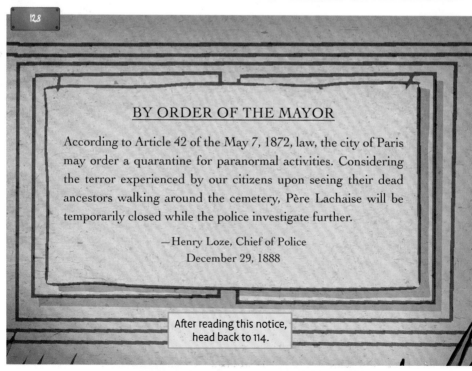

128

BY ORDER OF THE MAYOR

According to Article 42 of the May 7, 1872, law, the city of Paris may order a quarantine for paranormal activities. Considering the terror experienced by our citizens upon seeing their dead ancestors walking around the cemetery, Père Lachaise will be temporarily closed while the police investigate further.

—Henry Loze, Chief of Police
December 29, 1888

After reading this notice, head back to 114.

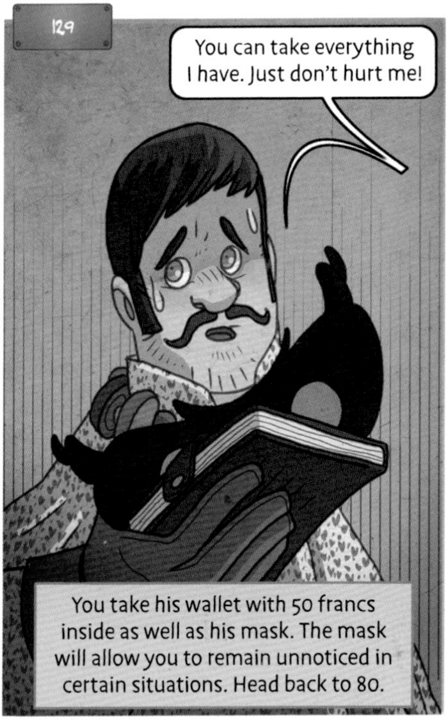
129
You can take everything I have. Just don't hurt me!
You take his wallet with 50 francs inside as well as his mask. The mask will allow you to remain unnoticed in certain situations. Head back to 80.

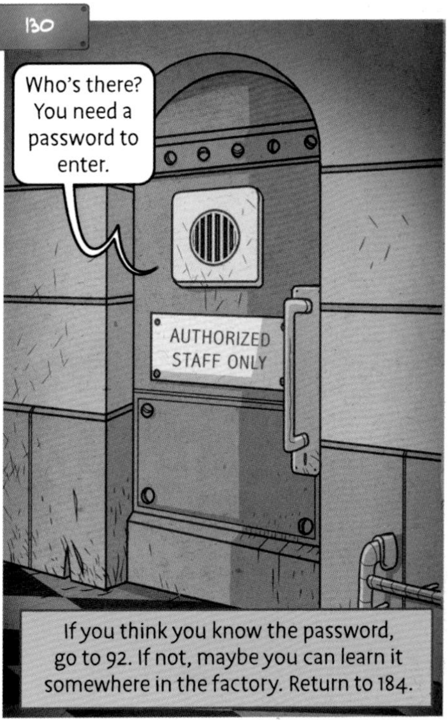
130
Who's there? You need a password to enter.
AUTHORIZED STAFF ONLY
If you think you know the password, go to 92. If not, maybe you can learn it somewhere in the factory. Return to 184.

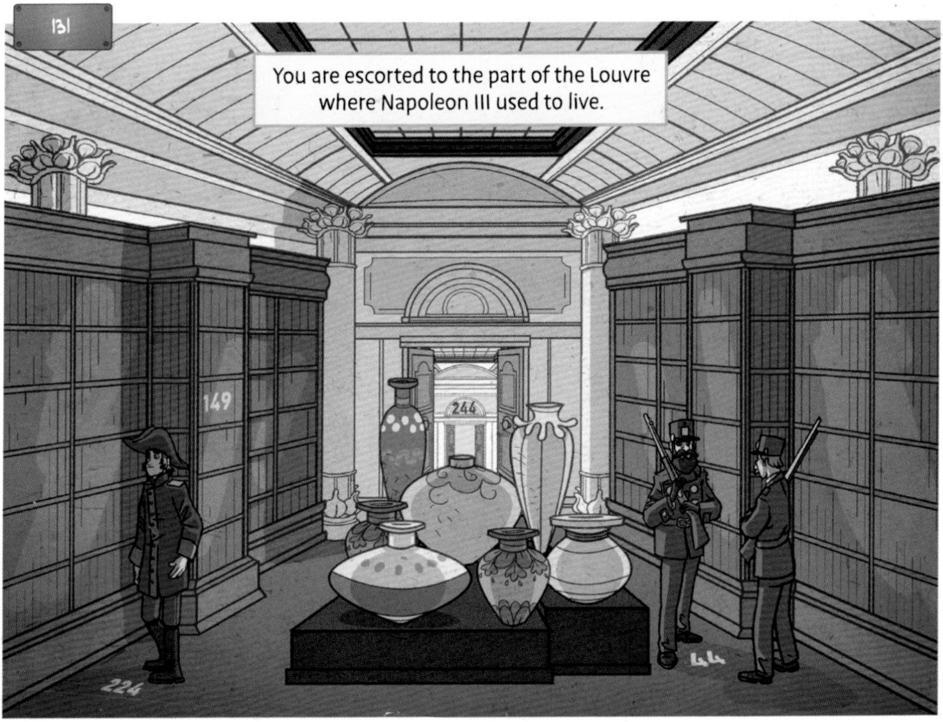
131
You are escorted to the part of the Louvre where Napoleon III used to live.
149
244
224
44

This entrance has been walled off. If you want to break through, you'll have to identify the loose bricks by solving the puzzle. Fill in each empty square with a number between 1 and 6. Each number can appear only once in each line, column, and square. After you've solved it, head to 116.

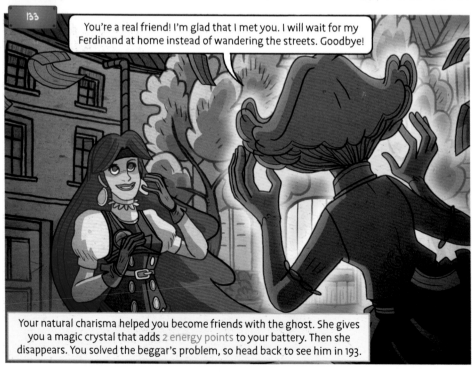

You're a real friend! I'm glad that I met you. I will wait for my Ferdinand at home instead of wandering the streets. Goodbye!

Your natural charisma helped you become friends with the ghost. She gives you a magic crystal that adds 2 energy points to your battery. Then she disappears. You solved the beggar's problem, so head back to see him in 193.

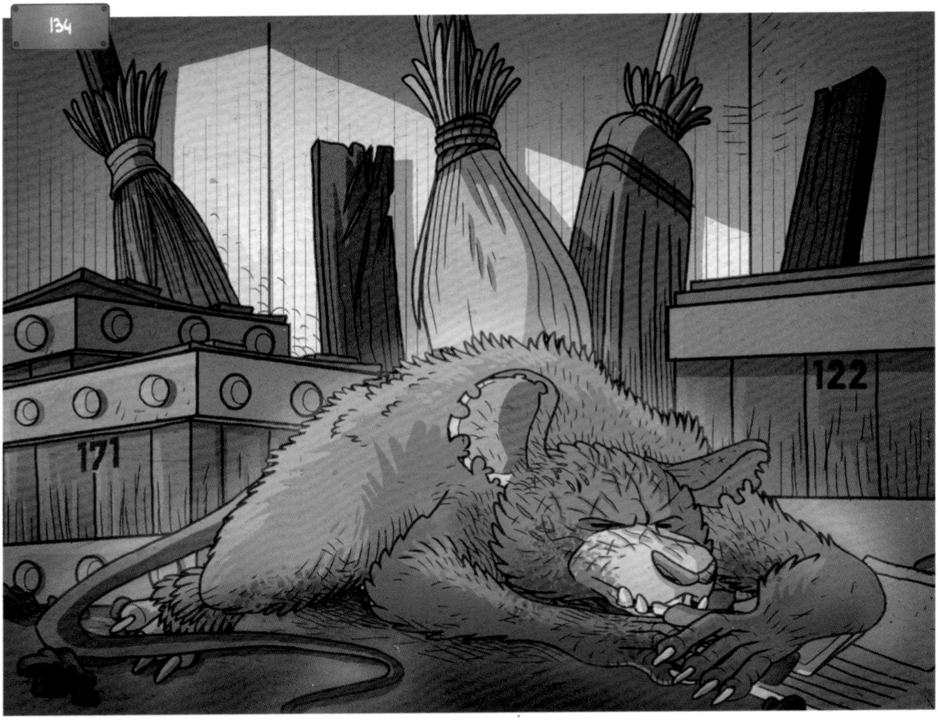
134
171
122

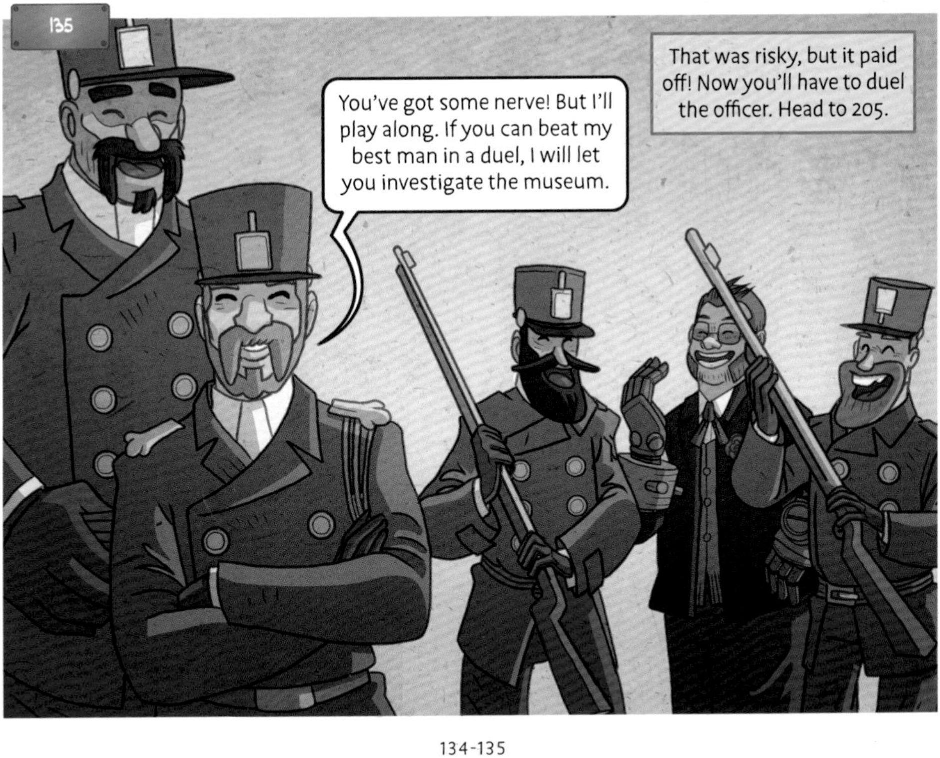
135
You've got some nerve! But I'll play along. If you can beat my best man in a duel, I will let you investigate the museum.
That was risky, but it paid off! Now you'll have to duel the officer. Head to 205.

136

You slowly awaken . . . but where are you? You've never seen this place before.

137

You've come to the right guy! I trust you. You can take the keys from my belt and leave them at reception when you're finished.

You take the keys to the warehouse and head back to 64.

138

Oh, that singer! She says she's been possessed by a ghost when she sings every night for the past two weeks. This is my first night singing with her, and I don't believe it. I think she's just trying to get attention.

You were allowed to ask him only one question. Now leave and return to 285.

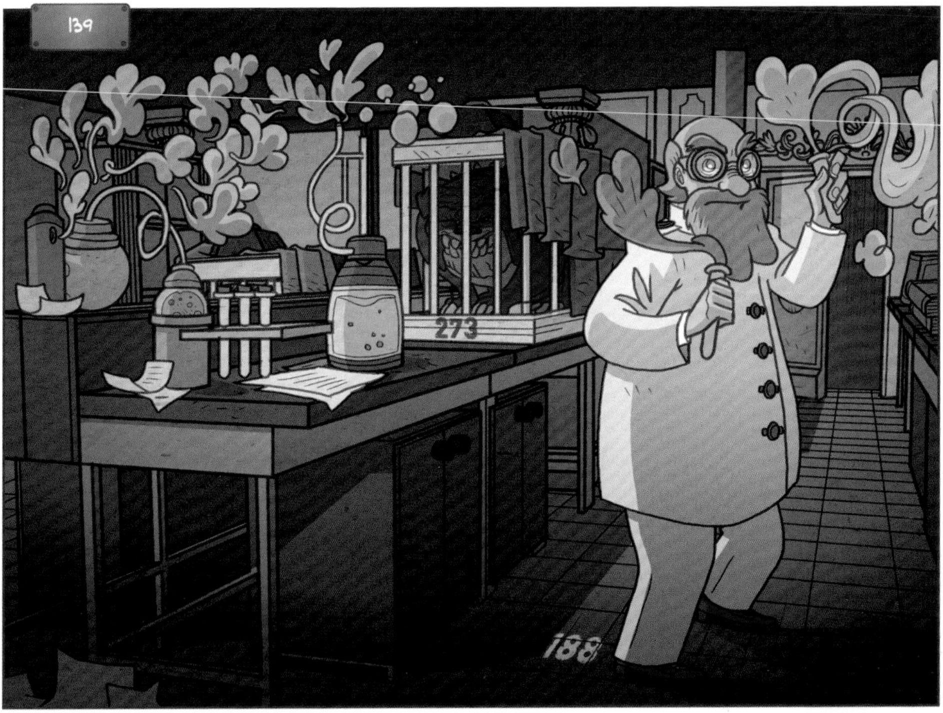
139
273
188

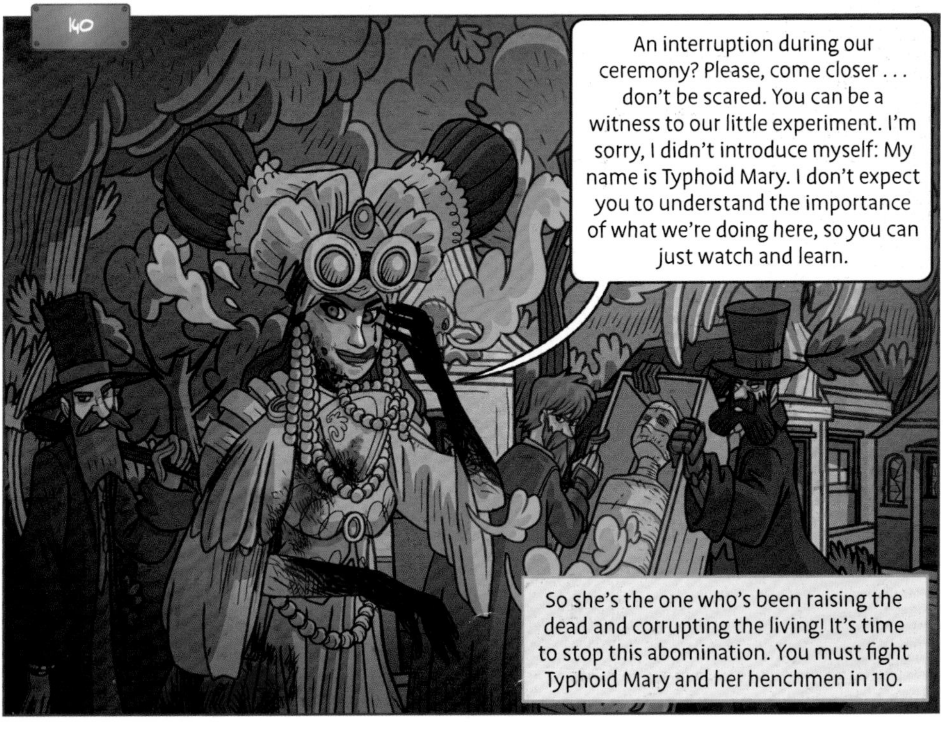
140
An interruption during our ceremony? Please, come closer . . . don't be scared. You can be a witness to our little experiment. I'm sorry, I didn't introduce myself: My name is Typhoid Mary. I don't expect you to understand the importance of what we're doing here, so you can just watch and learn.
So she's the one who's been raising the dead and corrupting the living! It's time to stop this abomination. You must fight Typhoid Mary and her henchmen in 110.

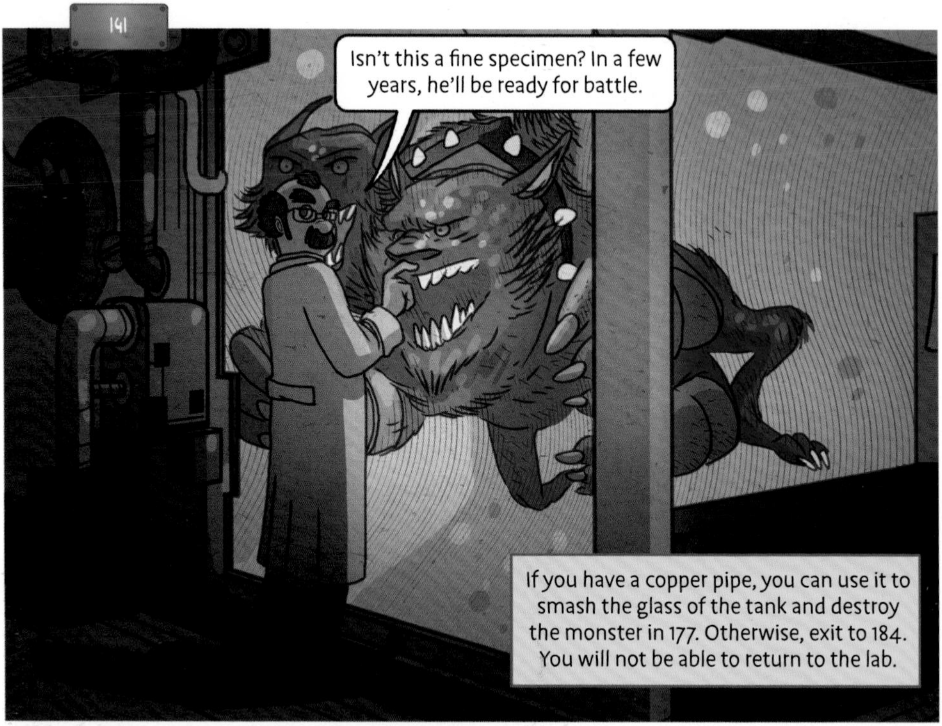
141
Isn't this a fine specimen? In a few years, he'll be ready for battle.
If you have a copper pipe, you can use it to smash the glass of the tank and destroy the monster in 177. Otherwise, exit to 184. You will not be able to return to the lab.

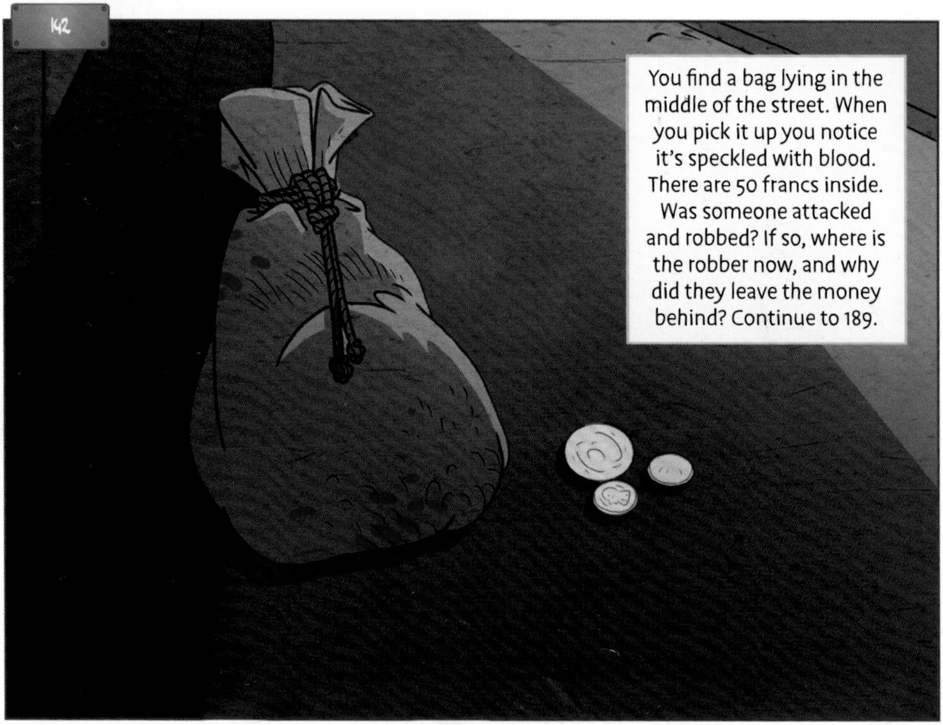
142
You find a bag lying in the middle of the street. When you pick it up you notice it's speckled with blood. There are 50 francs inside. Was someone attacked and robbed? If so, where is the robber now, and why did they leave the money behind? Continue to 189.

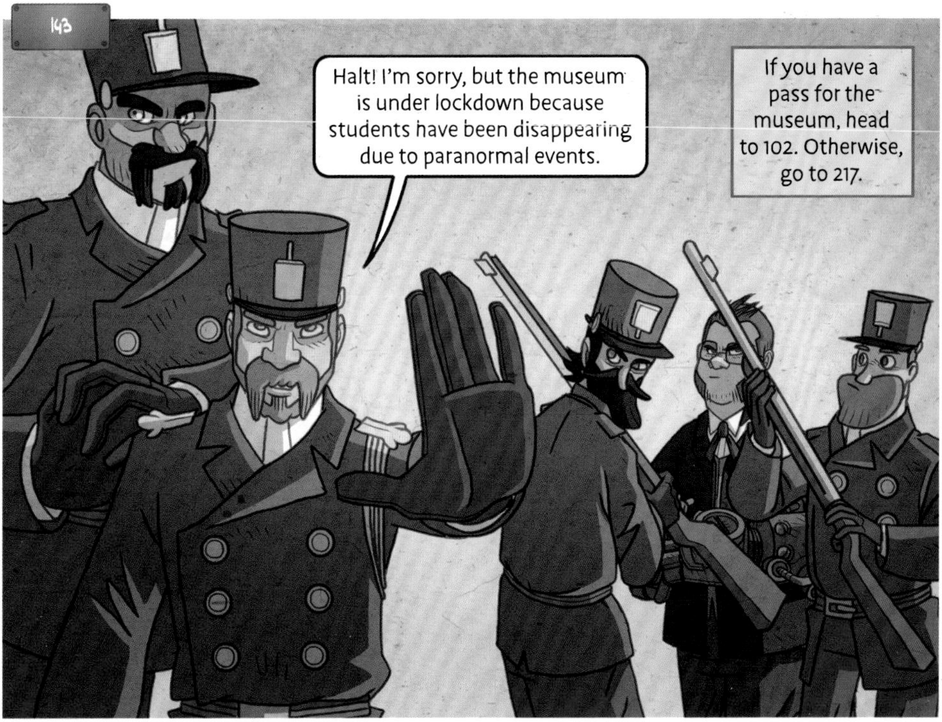
143
Halt! I'm sorry, but the museum is under lockdown because students have been disappearing due to paranormal events.
If you have a pass for the museum, head to 102. Otherwise, go to 217.

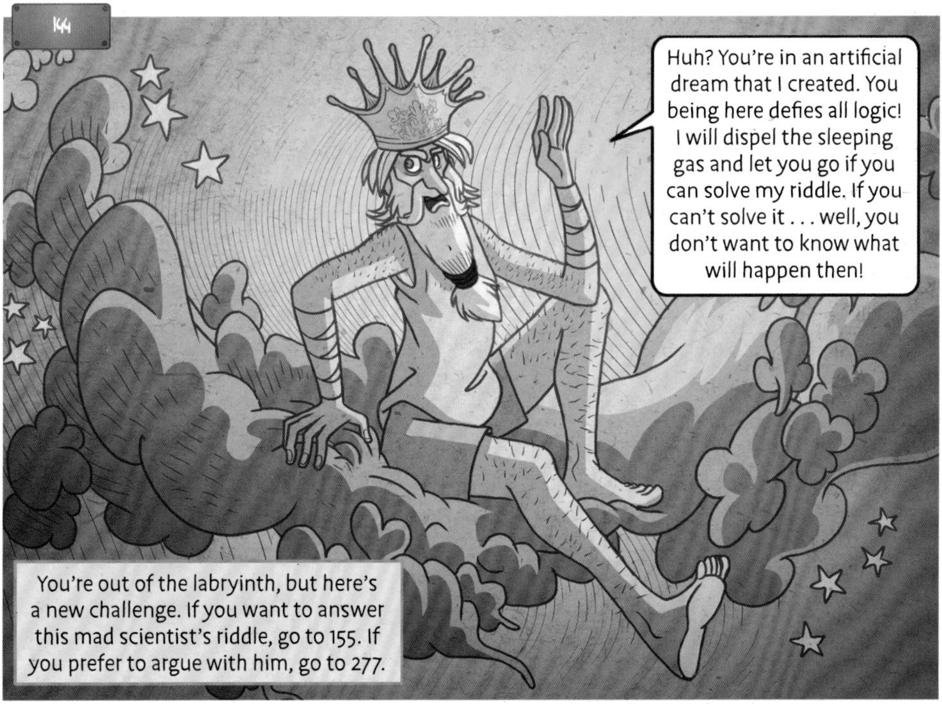
144
Huh? You're in an artificial dream that I created. You being here defies all logic! I will dispel the sleeping gas and let you go if you can solve my riddle. If you can't solve it . . . well, you don't want to know what will happen then!
You're out of the labryinth, but here's a new challenge. If you want to answer this mad scientist's riddle, go to 155. If you prefer to argue with him, go to 277.

CANNON DOG
Technology 7

Dodge the cannonballs and neutralize this guy, then continue to 306.

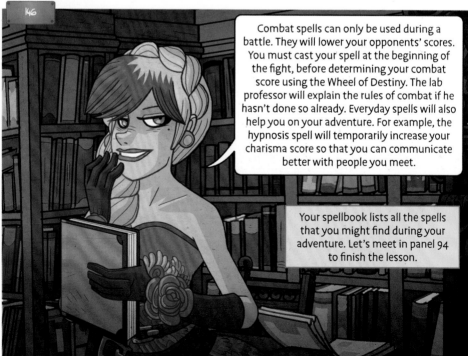

Combat spells can only be used during a battle. They will lower your opponents' scores. You must cast your spell at the beginning of the fight, before determining your combat score using the Wheel of Destiny. The lab professor will explain the rules of combat if he hasn't done so already. Everyday spells will also help you on your adventure. For example, the hypnosis spell will temporarily increase your charisma score so that you can communicate better with people you meet.

Your spellbook lists all the spells that you might find during your adventure. Let's meet in panel 94 to finish the lesson.

Please, can you spare any change?

If you want to help this man, give him 25 francs and head to 48. Otherwise, go back to 363.

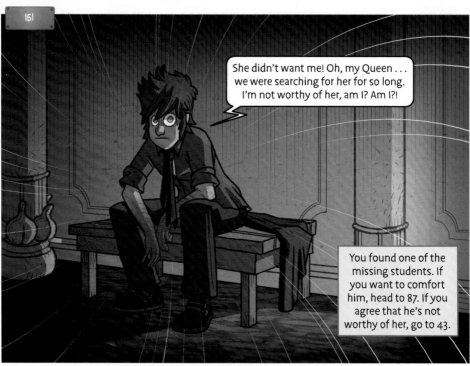

She didn't want me! Oh, my Queen . . . we were searching for her for so long. I'm not worthy of her, am I? Am I?!

You found one of the missing students. If you want to comfort him, head to 87. If you agree that he's not worthy of her, go to 43.

So what? You're not the first student to come to the museum to investigate. Mr. Eiffel can't do anything about it, unless . . .

If you have 4 or more charisma points, head to 253. Otherwise, go to 208.

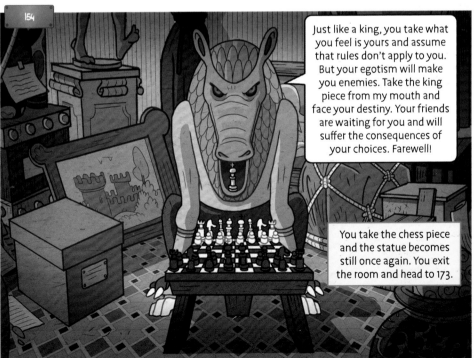

Just like a king, you take what you feel is yours and assume that rules don't apply to you. But your egotism will make you enemies. Take the king piece from my mouth and face your destiny. Your friends are waiting for you and will suffer the consequences of your choices. Farewell!

You take the chess piece and the statue becomes still once again. You exit the room and head to 173.

Very good, very good! Here is my riddle: Black within and red without, four corners round about. What am I?

Remember that this guy is crazy. Think outside the box, and you will find the solution to his riddle. Take your time, then head to 198.

A ghost?! Maybe this is the shadow the beggar was talking about. At the moment, he doesn't seem dangerous, so you gather your courage and go to meet him.

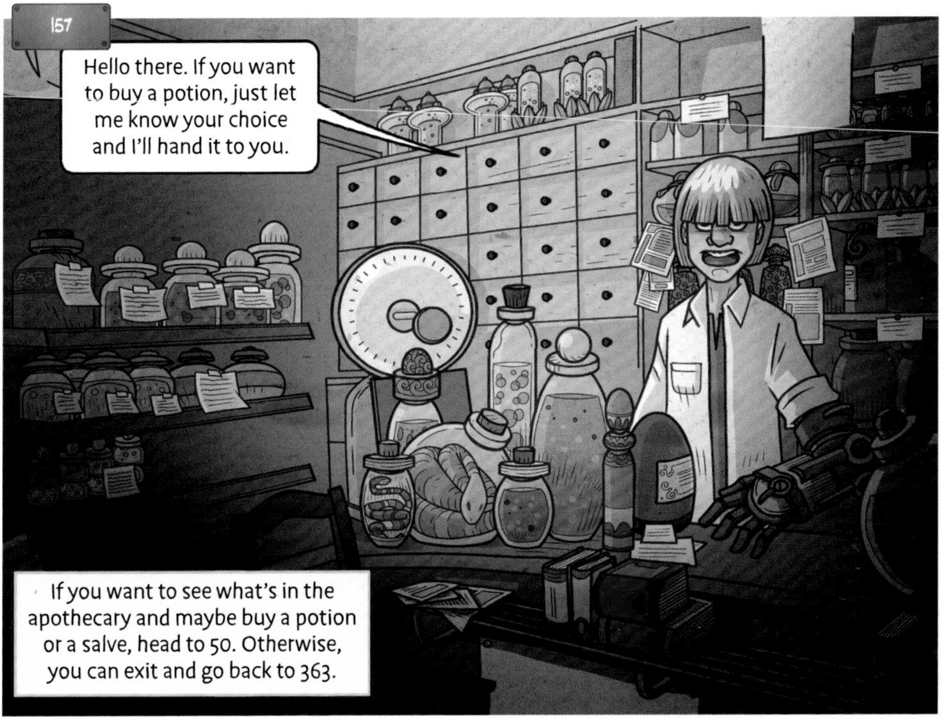
157
Hello there. If you want to buy a potion, just let me know your choice and I'll hand it to you.
If you want to see what's in the apothecary and maybe buy a potion or a salve, head to 50. Otherwise, you can exit and go back to 363.

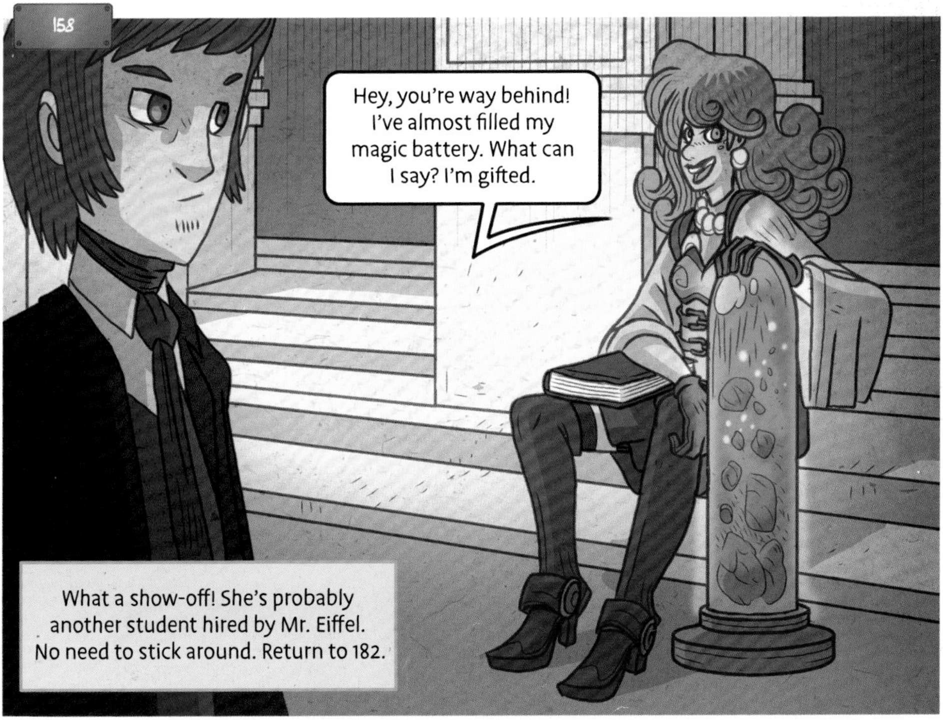
158
Hey, you're way behind! I've almost filled my magic battery. What can I say? I'm gifted.
What a show-off! She's probably another student hired by Mr. Eiffel. No need to stick around. Return to 182.

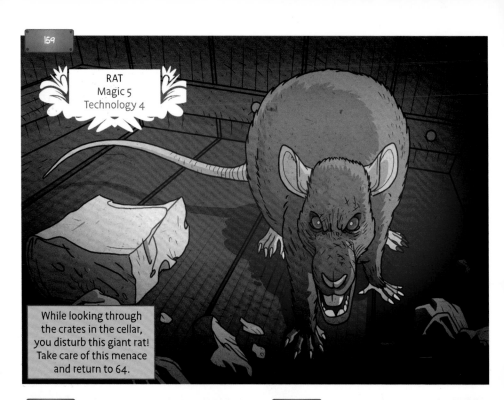

RAT
Magic 5
Technology 4

While looking through the crates in the cellar, you disturb this giant rat! Take care of this menace and return to 64.

CLACK

Click . . . click . . . ping! You cannot pick the lock or try again. Never mind—head back to 189. You won't be able to open this door, even with a weapon.

You used the cannon to shoot a crate of ammunition. The whole warehouse exploded . . . and you along with it. You are no more. Start the adventure over again.

Once the smoke has cleared, you notice with satisfaction that your precise shot has hit the mark. Enter the house in 385.

You search the skeleton and find a vampirism spell! If you've already been here, don't take the spell. Head back to 9.

So, another curious cat . . . I'll defeat you like I defeated that officer!

SPY
Magic 5
Technology 6

If you're able to beat this secret agent, head to 321.

167

You give a warm wave to the guard, who hands you your exit papers. Head back to 223.

168

The king wants. The madman rambles. The knight asks. The soldier stands. Only the one who has confronted them all and made a choice will be able to face the queen.

A woman's voice speaks to you through the door. If you think you've done what she asks, head to 284. Otherwise, continue your exploration by returning to 23. You will be able to return to this door when you're ready.

169

FACTORY DIRECTOR
Magic 3
Technology 4

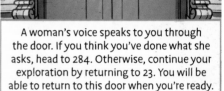

You'll never beat me!

Defeat this traitor, who has 100 francs in his wallet. Then search the room in 347.

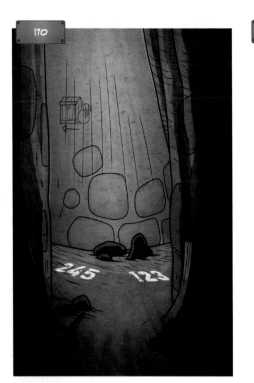

You find a vitality spell in the box. The show is starting soon, so you don't have time to explore the room any further. You return to 61.

HANSEL AND GRETEL
Magic 5
Technology 4

Hansel and Gretel are steaming mad! Luckily, the door behind them seems to be the way out of this horrible maze.

After meeting Ammit, you head back the way you came to dissipate the mysterious force field from the Louvre corridor. If you have the rook in your hand, go to 308. If you have the knight, go to 150. If you have the king, go to 355.

TYPHOID MARY
Magic 8
Technology 4

Typhoid Mary spits poisonous vapors at you, lowering both your technology and magic scores by 1 point each for this fight! If you are able to beat her, head to 125.

After spending a few hours in the Père Lachaise Cemetery, you come across a strange gathering at dusk . . .

For now, they don't see you. If you have a lady's or a gentleman's outfit, you may try to infiltrate the group in 214. Otherwise, move on to 140.

What have you done? No . . . Ahhhh!

You have destroyed the factory's secret project. Now, quickly exit the factory in 199.

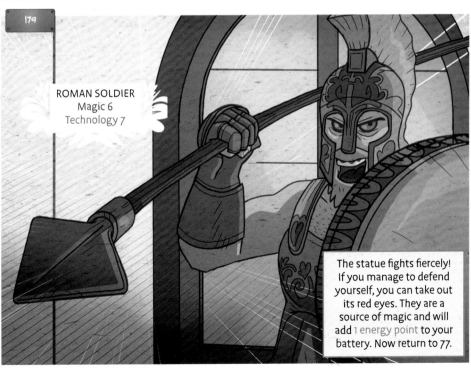

ROMAN SOLDIER
Magic 6
Technology 7

The statue fights fiercely! If you manage to defend yourself, you can take out its red eyes. They are a source of magic and will add 1 energy point to your battery. Now return to 77.

Nice shot! Take advantage of the chaos and move quickly.

152

Thank you for not attacking me. I may have come back from the dead—I still don't know why—but I do have a conscience! To thank you for your kindness, I will give you some advice. Be careful at the crypts a little farther on; they are booby-trapped. If given a choice, always take the right-hand path once you're inside.

A little civility in this decomposing world is always appreciated. Head back to 104.

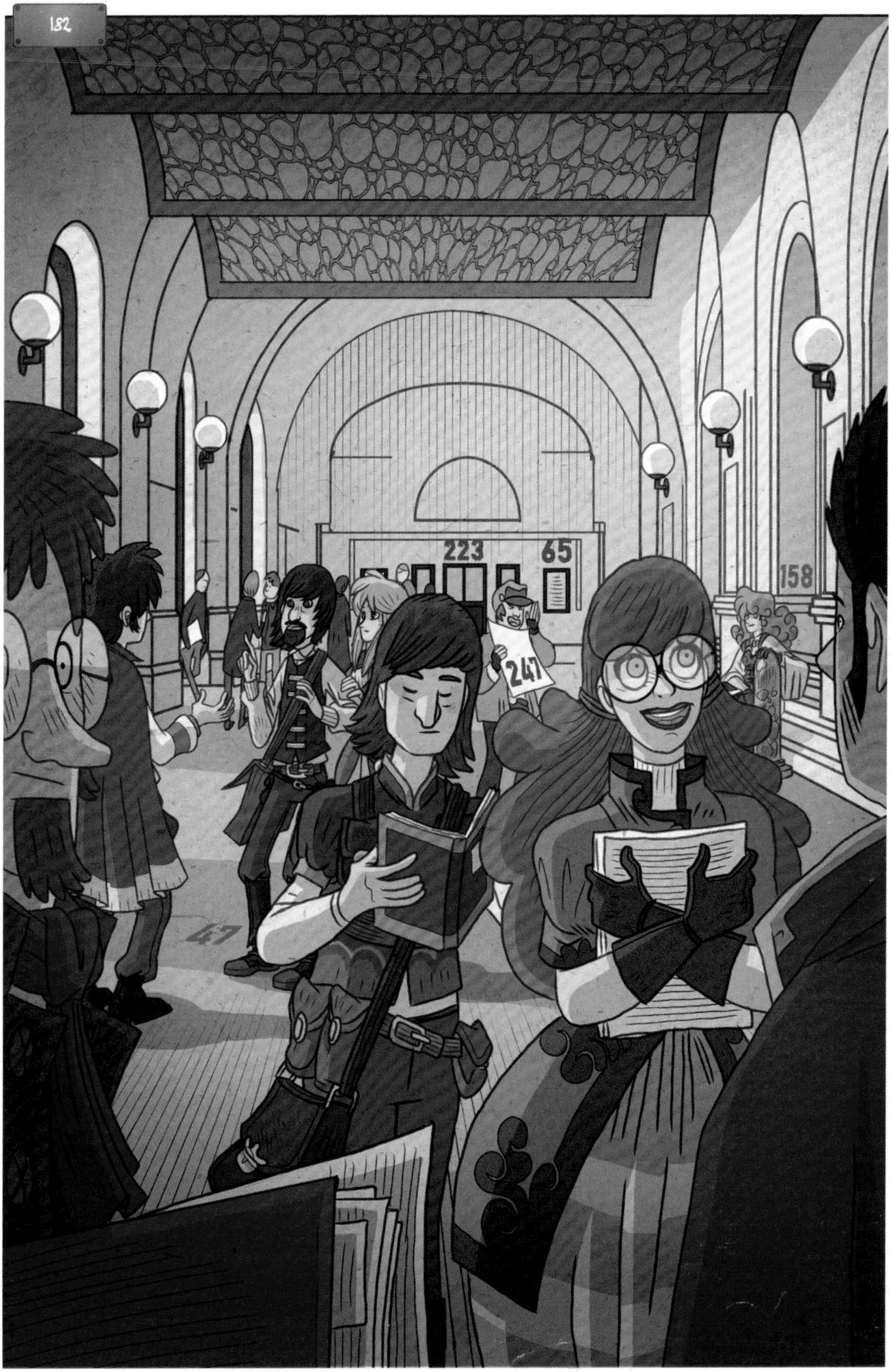
223
65
158
247
47

A sudden dizziness overpowers you. Your head is spinning . . . If your character is a girl, you faint in 136. If your character is a boy, you faint in 272.

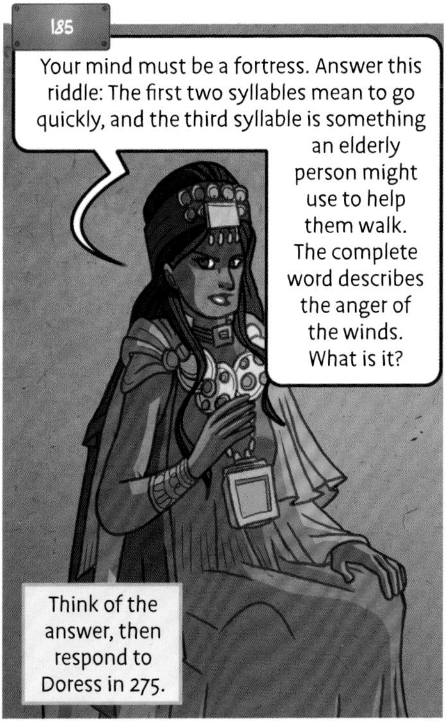
185
Your mind must be a fortress. Answer this riddle: The first two syllables mean to go quickly, and the third syllable is something an elderly person might use to help them walk. The complete word describes the anger of the winds. What is it?
Think of the answer, then respond to Doress in 275.

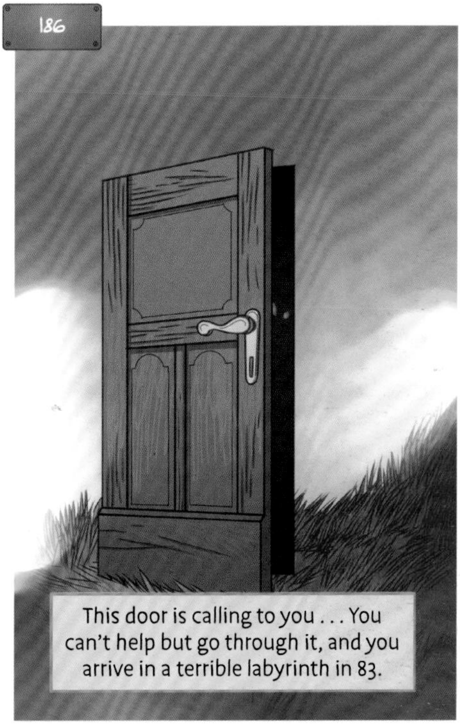
186
This door is calling to you . . . You can't help but go through it, and you arrive in a terrible labyrinth in 83.

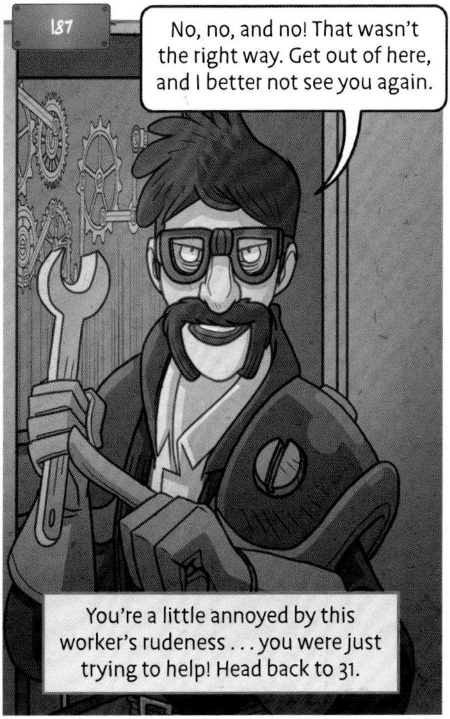
187
No, no, and no! That wasn't the right way. Get out of here, and I better not see you again.
You're a little annoyed by this worker's rudeness . . . you were just trying to help! Head back to 31.

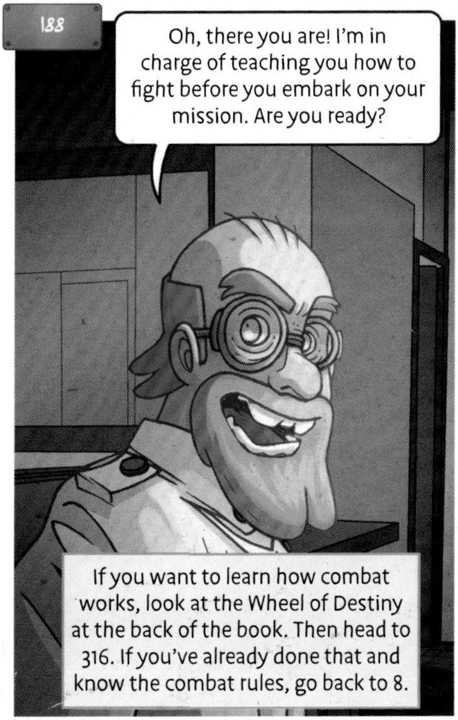
188
Oh, there you are! I'm in charge of teaching you how to fight before you embark on your mission. Are you ready?
If you want to learn how combat works, look at the Wheel of Destiny at the back of the book. Then head to 316. If you've already done that and know the combat rules, go back to 8.

Goldilocks and her bears want to eat you for dinner! If you've already come this way, you have to fight them again.

GOLDILOCKS
Magic 4

It's good you waited because that was a demon speaking through my mouth . . . and we figured out how to break the enchantment by ourselves. Thank you!

You learned Ammit's lesson. Instead of blindly obeying, you did what you thought was wisest. One of the students is named Simon. It's time to exit in 399.

Thank you, thank you! I owe you a lot. Because of you, I will be able to sleep soundly again. Here, a reward for you.

Because you helped rid the beggar of his nightmares, he hands you a magic crystal that adds 3 energy points to your battery! Now return to 363.

Of course, it's milk! That's the most logical answer.

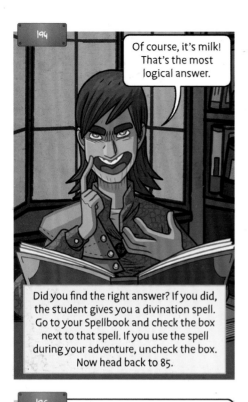

Did you find the right answer? If you did, the student gives you a divination spell. Go to your Spellbook and check the box next to that spell. If you use the spell during your adventure, uncheck the box. Now head back to 85.

A shabby student! The privilege of hearing an opera singer possessed by a ghost isn't for low-class people like you.

What a welcome committee . . . If you have 7 or more charisma points, you can answer him in 246. Otherwise, return to 209.

We work hard, but the pay is great! Honestly, though, it scares me what they do in the lab . . . Sometimes we hear inhuman screams coming from there.

After talking to the worker, you return to 184.

This door is locked. If you have something to open it with, head to 115. You can also try using a weapon in 358. Otherwise, go back to 189.

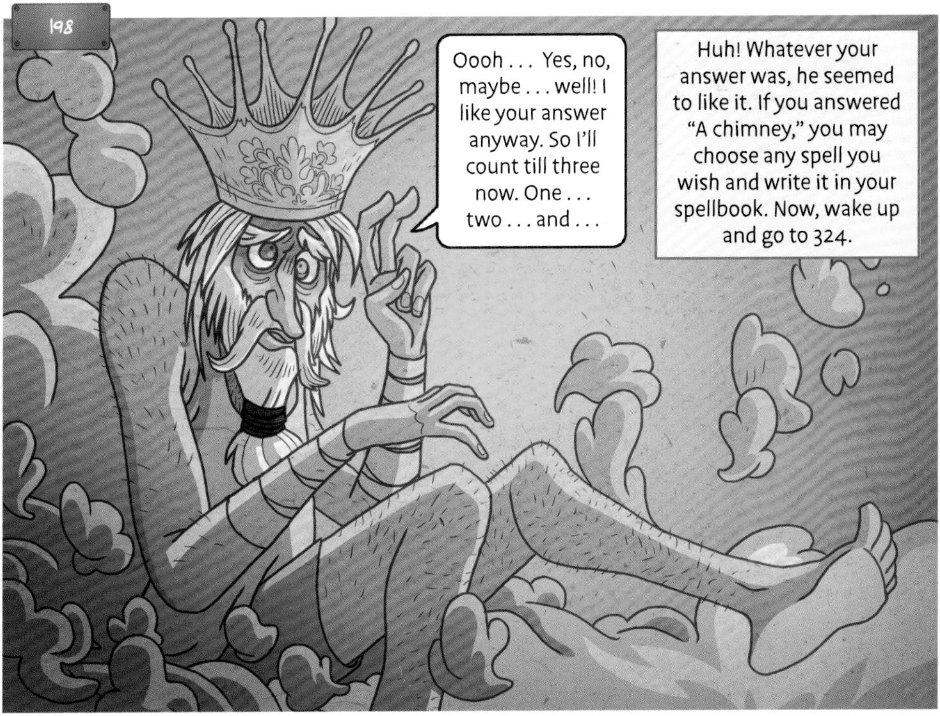
198
Oooh . . . Yes, no, maybe . . . well! I like your answer anyway. So I'll count till three now. One . . . two . . . and . . .
Huh! Whatever your answer was, he seemed to like it. If you answered "A chimney," you may choose any spell you wish and write it in your spellbook. Now, wake up and go to 324.

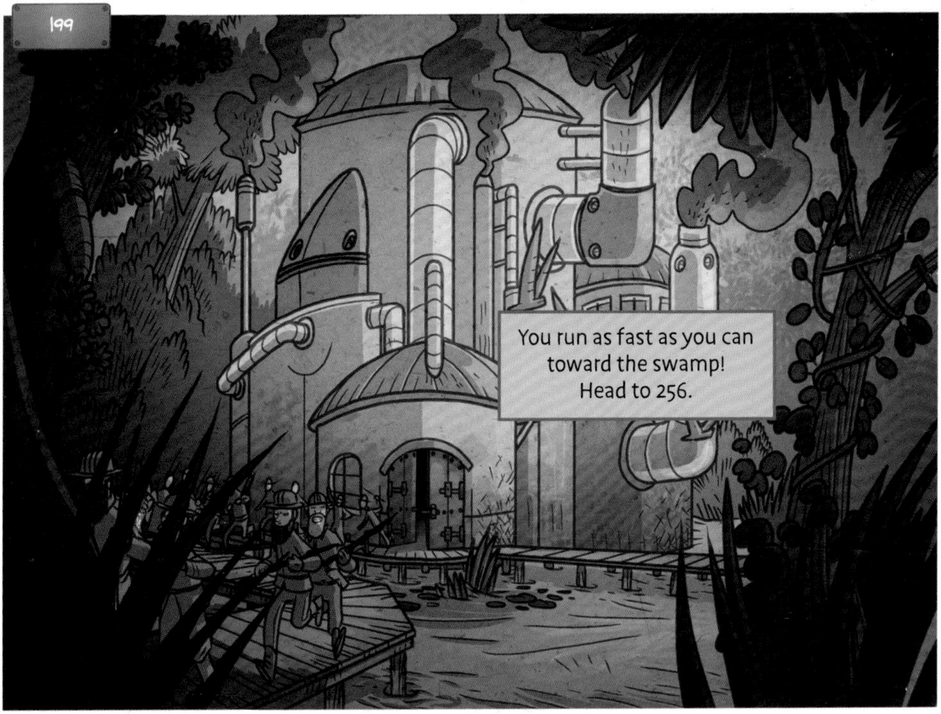
199
You run as fast as you can toward the swamp! Head to 256.

200

This door is locked and it's impossible to pick it. If you found the key in the factory, open it in 237. Otherwise, head back to 31.

201

You see an abandoned bag. If you want to look through it, go to 344. If you prefer to leave it with the attendant without opening it, head to 287.

202

She's a meanie! I don't want to become like her. Mary said everything would be better, but it isn't true!

This poor little girl seems very sick. You will take care of her at another time. Continue to 298.

203

This filing cabinet has three drawers, all unlocked. You may also return to the director's office in 60.

124

113

97

One night on stage, I felt a lightheadedness that lasted for a few moments. Then it was like a waking dream . . . I was singing, but I wasn't myself anymore. At the end of the show, I returned to my senses. Then I learned that people saw a ghost floating around my head! It's been like this for two weeks.

Interesting. You thank the opera singer, and she gives you a backstage pass. Go backstage in 212.

OFFICER
Magic 8
Technology 7

Big guy! Once you win the duel, return to the commanding officer in 119.

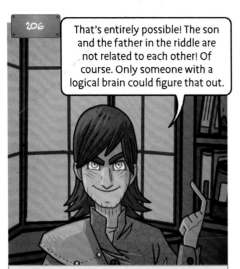

206

That's entirely possible! The son and the father in the riddle are not related to each other! Of course. Only someone with a logical brain could figure that out.

Did you get the right answer? If you did, the student gives you a divination spell as a reward. Go to your Spellbook and check one of the two boxes next to that spell. If you use the spell during your adventure, uncheck the box, just as you would for any other spell. Head back to 85.

207

What a surprise! If you have any money, I recommend the Halles Mall nearby to get yourself some nice clothes.

What a coincidence to see Gustave Eiffel again. You look at your map to continue to your chosen destination. Or you can follow his advice and head to 363.

208

The officer will let you in only if you prove your wits.

Let's see if you have a sense of humor. Answer me this: How many tickles does it take to make an octopus laugh?

If you answer five, go to 75. If you answer ten, go to 71.

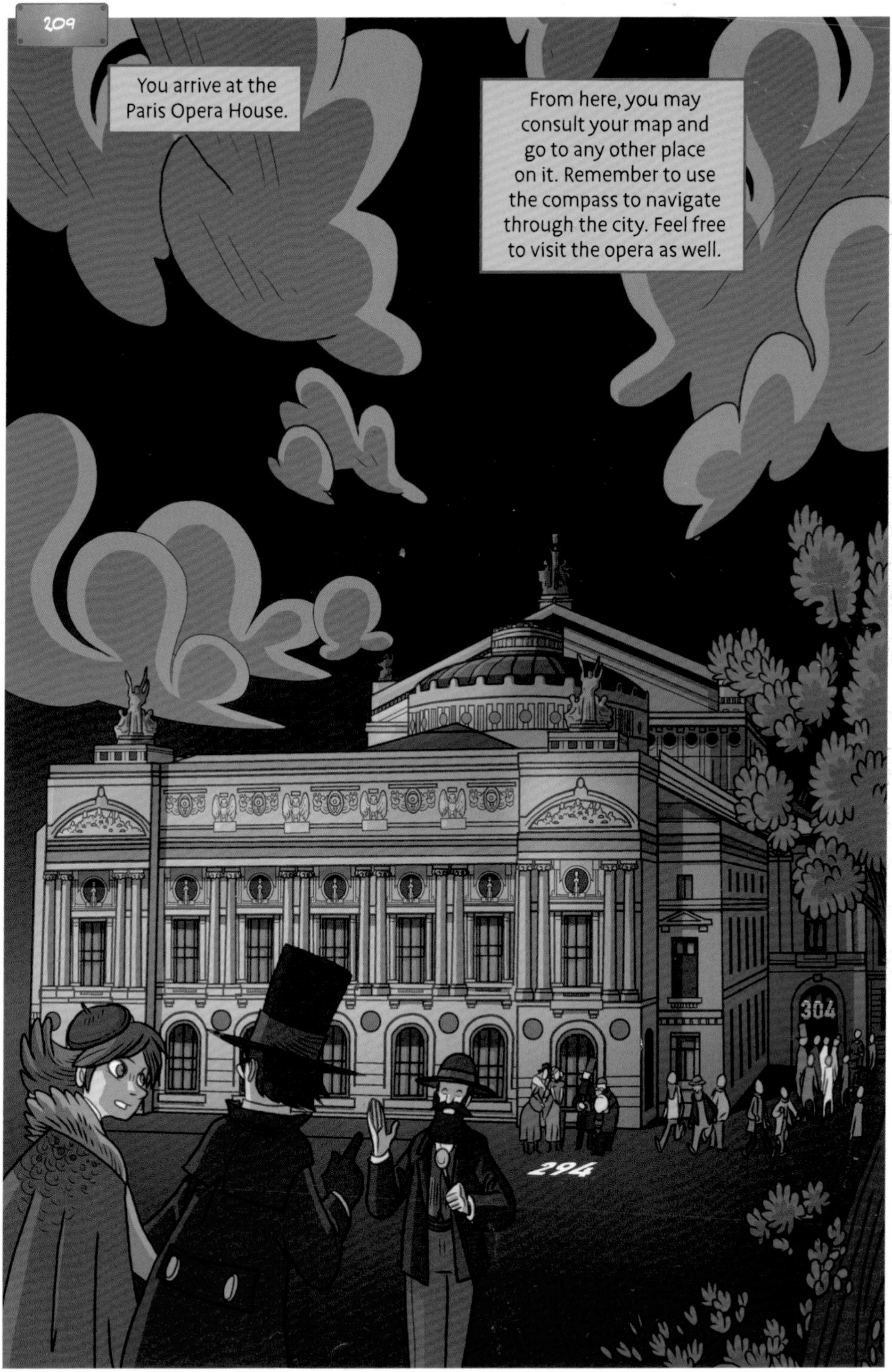
209
You arrive at the Paris Opera House.
From here, you may consult your map and go to any other place on it. Remember to use the compass to navigate through the city. Feel free to visit the opera as well.
304
294

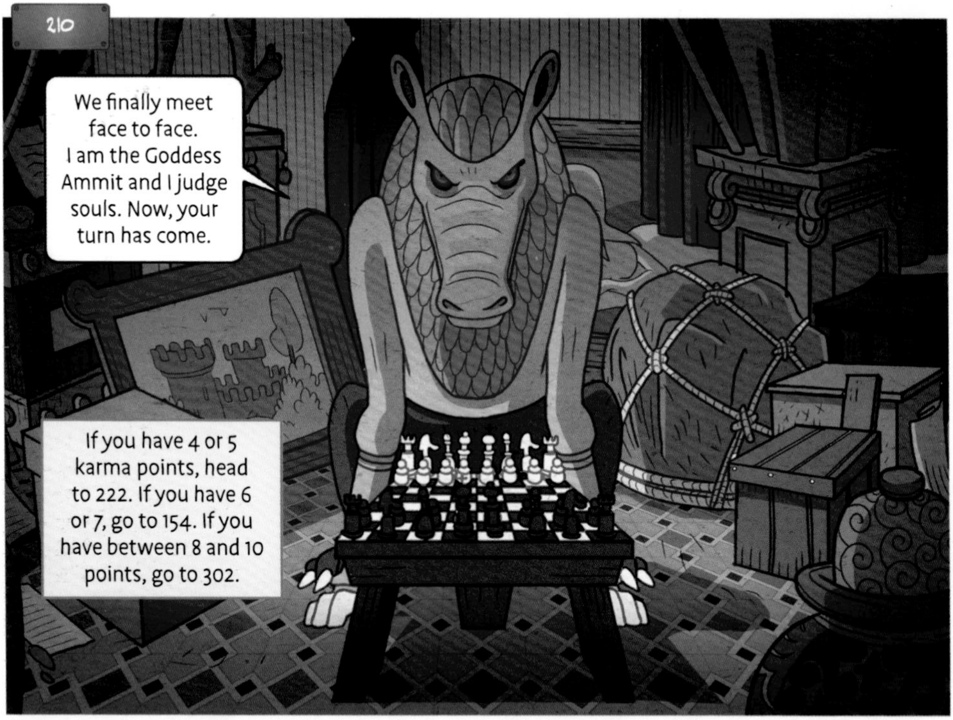
210
We finally meet face to face. I am the Goddess Ammit and I judge souls. Now, your turn has come.
If you have 4 or 5 karma points, head to 222. If you have 6 or 7, go to 154. If you have between 8 and 10 points, go to 302.

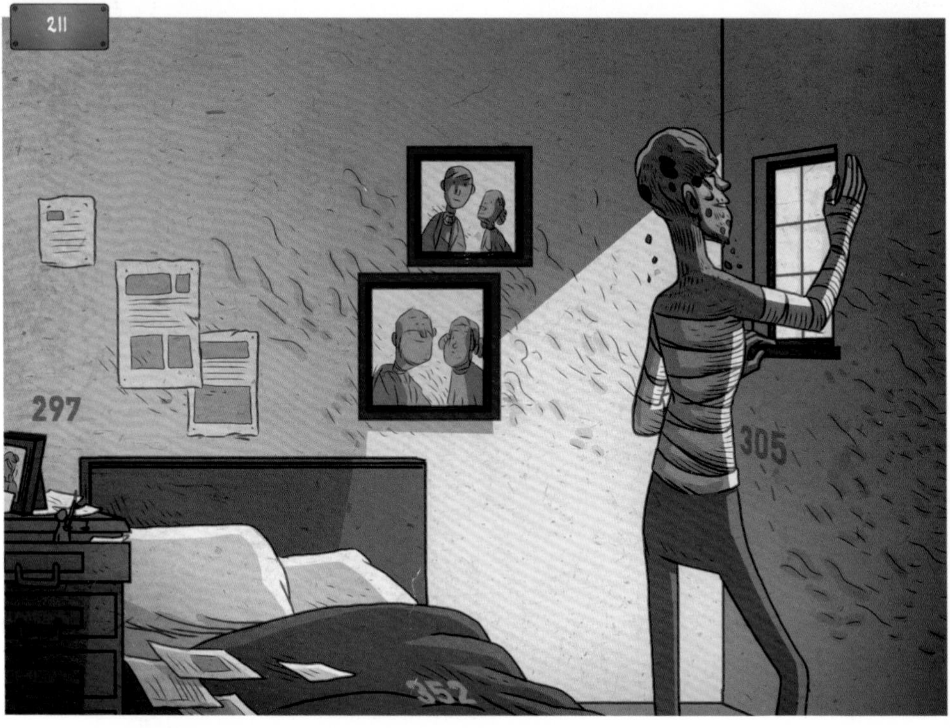
211
297
305
352

There are spies everywhere in this industry. You put down the file and head back to 60.

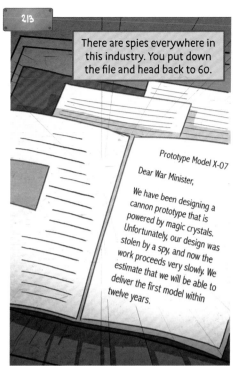

Prototype Model X-07

Dear War Minister,

We have been designing a cannon prototype that is powered by magic crystals. Unfortunately, our design was stolen by a spy, and now the work proceeds very slowly. We estimate that we will be able to deliver the first model within twelve years.

You have successfully infiltrated the group. While a sickly looking woman leans toward the coffin, you have an opportunity to attack and take her by surprise in 175. If you'd rather wait, head to 140.

I am the watchtower rising against the enemy. Anyone who hesitates before acting does not have the soul of a conqueror!

This statue doesn't like that you're just standing there. If you want to teach it a lesson, go to 179. If you want to ignore it, return to 77. If you do, you won't be able to ask it any more questions.

GIANT RAT
Magic 6
Technology 5

A monstrous and misshapen rat attacks you as soon as you enter the storeroom! After defeating it, you can search the room in 134.

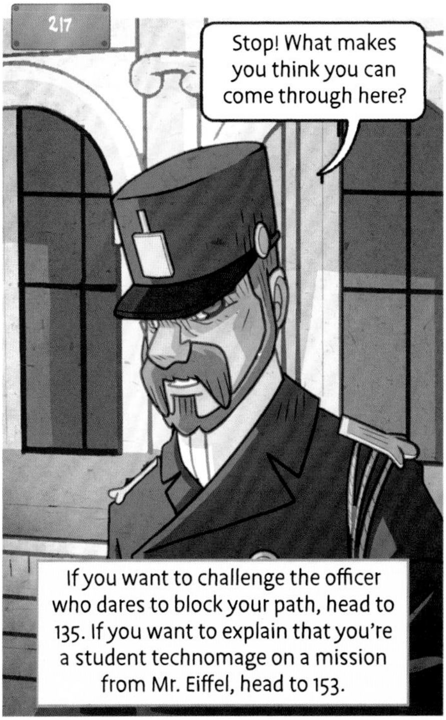
217
Stop! What makes you think you can come through here?
If you want to challenge the officer who dares to block your path, head to 135. If you want to explain that you're a student technomage on a mission from Mr. Eiffel, head to 153.

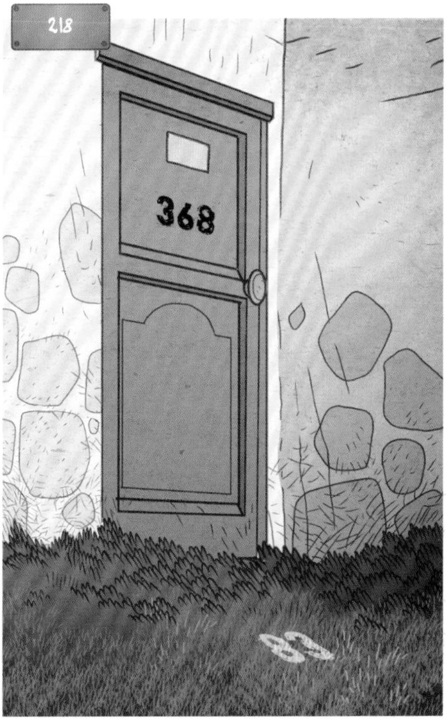
218
368
83

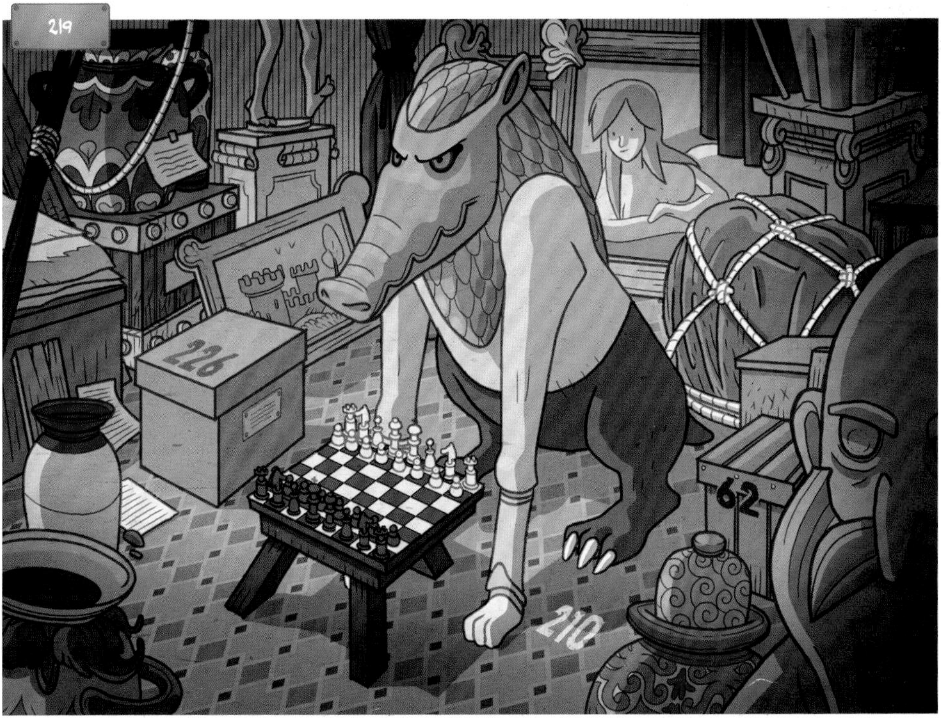
219
226
62
210

Is that a shape-shifting demon? You thought they existed only in legends! Even if you manage to defeat it, it will swallow 50 francs from your wallet as well as a spell scroll (you can decide which one) if you have both of those things. Now that it's cleaned you out, head to 84.

222

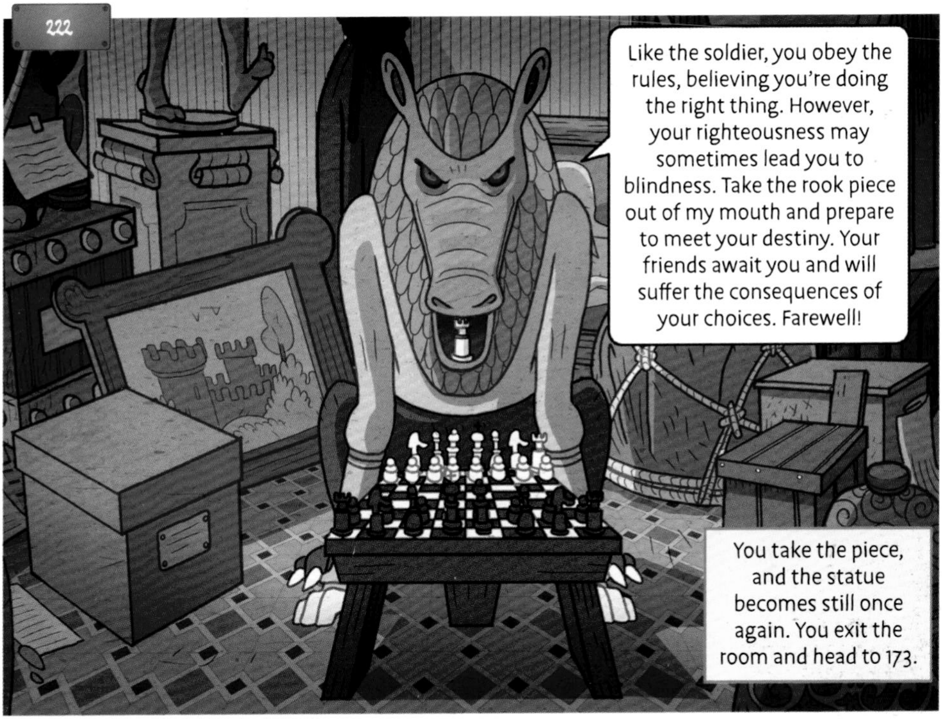
Like the soldier, you obey the rules, believing you're doing the right thing. However, your righteousness may sometimes lead you to blindness. Take the rook piece out of my mouth and prepare to meet your destiny. Your friends await you and will suffer the consequences of your choices. Farewell!
You take the piece, and the statue becomes still once again. You exit the room and head to 173.

223

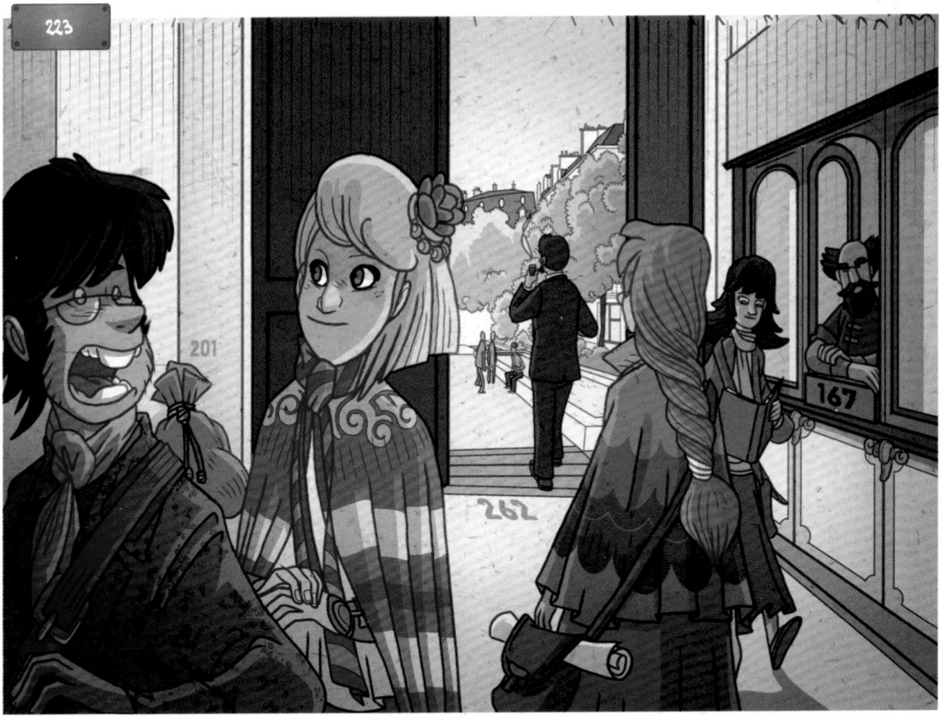
201
262
167

224

I'll admit that I'm scared to go any farther. This whole wing is cursed, do you hear me? Cursed! The artworks talk, I tell you! Yes, they speak! I'm not crazy . . . I've seen it!

The museum curator seems terrified by whatever is beyond this room . . . Return to 131.

225

Listen, kid, I have better things to do than chat. If you want to help, we'll see if you're as smart as you say. Here's the logic problem I need to solve. If you answer it correctly, I'll give you a reward.

I come from the flesh and can turn without moving. What am I?

Come up with your answer, and then go to 194.

226

In the box, you find an alchemy spell as well as an illusion spell! Now head back to the Egyptian statue in 210.

227

Don't hurt me! I'll tell you everything! I am the director of the factory, and I sold our secrets to a foreign power. Have pity on me!

Shameful. If you want to challenge him to a duel, head to 169. If you'd rather deliver him to the authorities, head to 235.

228

I am the witness to violence; I obey even though I am terrified. I carry the dual symbol of death and labor, but what I am looking for is the weapon that can strike from both sides. If you can correct this mistake, the curse will be lifted.

This soldier seems haunted by the past. Head back to 178.

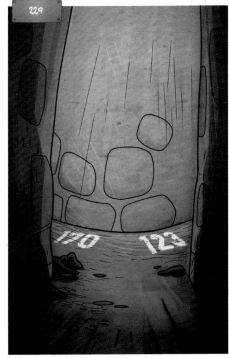

229

You can now decide where to go next on the Paris map. But before you go, look at the circle on the last page if you haven't already. This is your compass. You can either spin a crayon or toss a small object (like a coin) and see which number it lands on or closest to. (You may also use a single die instead of the wheel. Assign each side of the die to a panel number on the compass.) Go to the number you get and see what you find. This represents your travels on your way to your destination. After that, you may go to your original destination on the map.

In summary, you use the Wheel of Destiny during combat to determine your score as well as the score of your enemy. You use the compass to move across Paris. Every time you choose a destination on the map, you must first use the compass and go to the number indicated before heading to your destination. Now go to 67 to finish your conversation with Mr. Eiffel.

That shot didn't do anything except alert the factory's security guards! You have time for one more shot before you're stopped. Shoot the door in 180 or shoot the boxes in 161.

DO NOT OPEN WITHOUT AUTHORIZATION

232

This underground path leads you to a magic crystal! It adds 2 energy points to your battery. You then exit the house onto the street in 37.

233

Very good! What did you bring me?

A band . . . you can give him a ring or a friendly army. If you have the ring, head to 348. If you have the army, head to 364. If you have neither, return to 244 and you will be able to come back to this painting if you find either of these items later.

234

Not very subtle. At least you got to practice your aim. But the noise may have attracted some unwanted attention. You turn around and find yourself face to face with . . . well, go see in 166.

Oh, thank you for sparing me! You see, I have debts, and my daughter is very sick . . . that's why I became a traitor. You are a technomage, right? You can have anything you want in this room!

You tie up the factory director and then search the room in 380.

You want to talk to the opera singer, too? We can't figure out the password to get in to see her. But here's a hint: I have two hands upon my face and you check on me to keep your pace. What am I?

This sounds like the second part of a riddle. The solution will be the password you need in order to enter the opera singer's dressing room. Return to 255.

The show will start in a few minutes, but instead of mingling with the other guests, try to find a way backstage. If there's a ghost in this place, that's where it'll be.

SPY
Magic 7
Technology 6

A spy attacks you! Defeat him, and then face the other man in 227.

I am happy to accept your help. You can try to calm the patients—they are anxious today. Then we will meet in the lab.

You now have access to Doctor Charcot's patients. Head back to 341. You won't be able to return to his office.

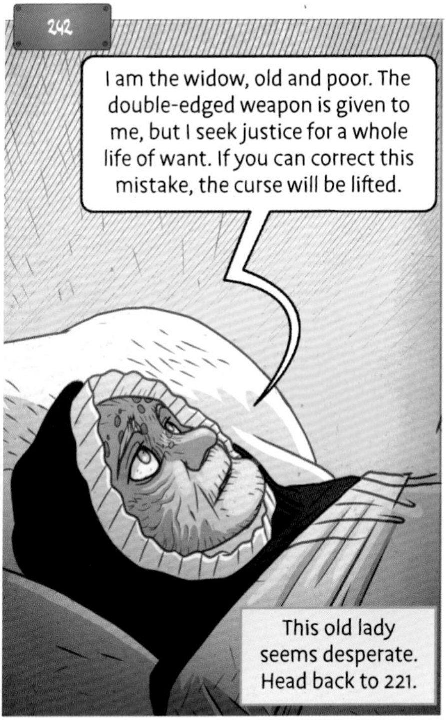
242
I am the widow, old and poor. The double-edged weapon is given to me, but I seek justice for a whole life of want. If you can correct this mistake, the curse will be lifted.
This old lady seems desperate. Head back to 221.

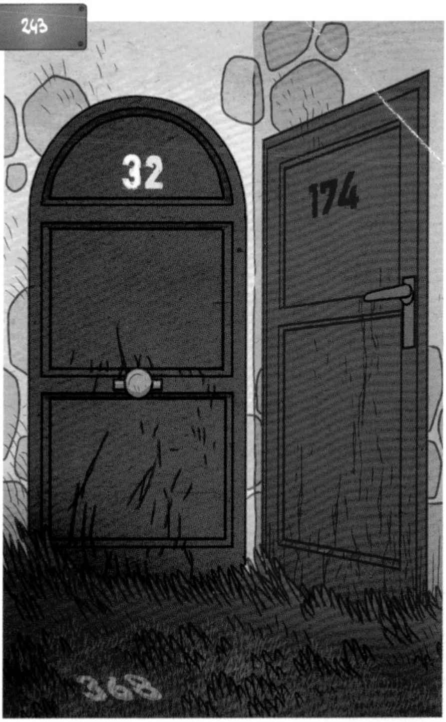
243
32
174
368

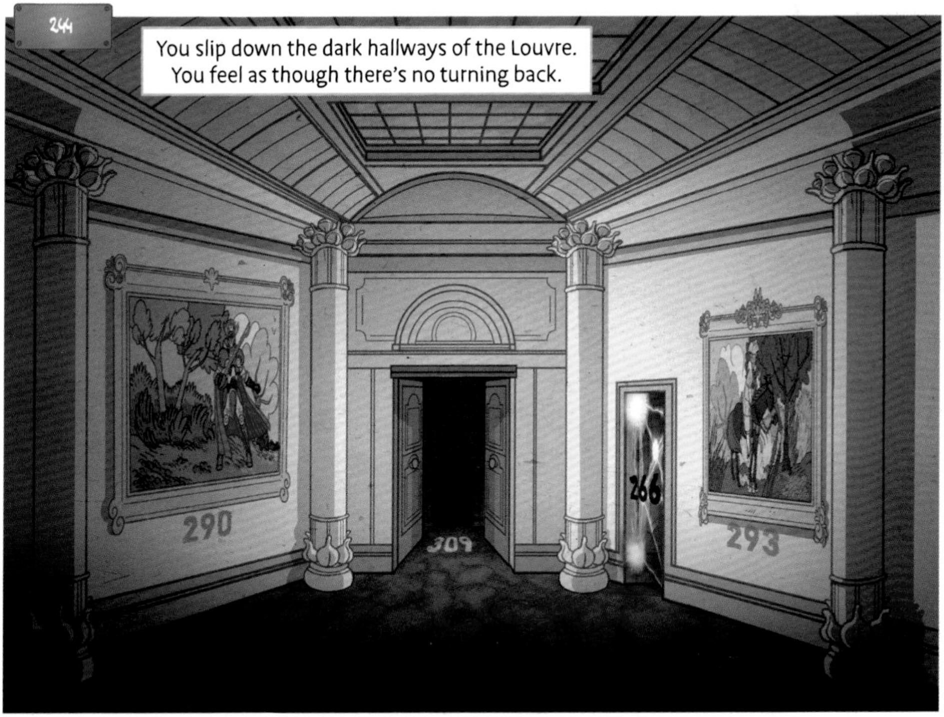
244
You slip down the dark hallways of the Louvre. You feel as though there's no turning back.
290
309
266
293

245

What carelessness! You fall into a boobytrap that kills you instantly! Start your adventure over again.

246

Oh, ho! What a clever comeback! We misjudged you. We have an extra ticket for tonight's show . . . I think you deserve it.

Well done! With this ticket, you can see the show tonight. Now return to 209.

247

Stuuudents loooost in the Louuuvre! Reeead allll abooout it!

University News

Strange Disappearances at the Louvre

Third-year students in archeowitchery disappeared during a visit to the Louvre last Saturday. University management refuses to comment. We demand an explanation!

Weapons Factory Is Hiring

The weapons factory is welcoming students for summer jobs at their branch in the Boulogne Swamp. Good health is required, as the vapors from the swamp are likely to irritate the lungs.

You take the flyer, then quickly head away from the yelling. Return to 182.

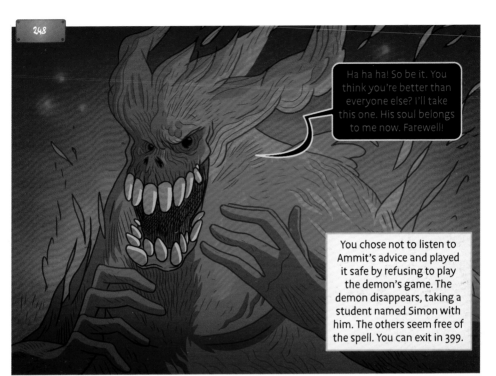

Ha ha ha! So be it. You think you're better than everyone else? I'll take this one. His soul belongs to me now. Farewell!

You chose not to listen to Ammit's advice and played it safe by refusing to play the demon's game. The demon disappears, taking a student named Simon with him. The others seem free of the spell. You can exit in 399.

Sure thing! I appreciate anyone smart enough to solve my riddles. It's one of my whims as a famous opera singer, I'm told. Here's a costume that will allow you to go backstage. But please don't bother me while I sing.

You thank the opera singer. Put on your costume and head backstage in 212.

250

YOU WHO VISIT MY FINAL RESTING PLACE, TAKE THE ROAD BENEATH YOUR FEET, CONTINUE ON YOUR LEFT WITHOUT FEAR, AND DISCOVER YOUR DESTINY!

After reading the plaque, return to 14.

251

What a crazy idea, trying to pet a mad dog! You lose 1 life point. This wasn't a smart move, but in other situations, your recklessness might pay off. Go see your professor in 188.

252

We were about to do something awful! Thank you for opening our eyes.

To stop making selfish and brutal enemies was Ammit's lesson. You saved all the students, including Simon. They reward you with a potion that gives you 1 life point. Exit in 399.

253

You convinced me! You may enter the Louvre. But be careful—there are some strange things going on inside.

You enter the Louvre in 131.

Interesting. You talked back and dared to take the painting with you, or you answered politely and were dismissed. How did you conduct yourself with the soldier?

If you didn't hesitate and touched the statue's spear, the voice gives you 2 points. If you hesitated, the voice gives you 1 point. Add up your points, remember that number, and head to 404.

299

303

236

315

238

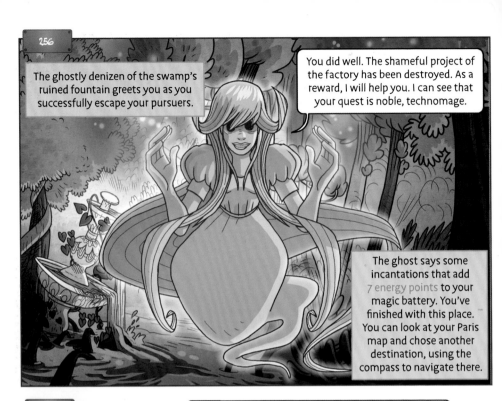

The ghostly denizen of the swamp's ruined fountain greets you as you successfully escape your pursuers.

You did well. The shameful project of the factory has been destroyed. As a reward, I will help you. I can see that your quest is noble, technomage.

The ghost says some incantations that add 7 energy points to your magic battery. You've finished with this place. You can look at your Paris map and chose another destination, using the compass to navigate there.

Don't judge me, I beg you. I belong to a secret society that meets in the cemetery at nightfall. Our group fell under the influence of woman named Mary Mallon.

Since then, everything has gone wrong! If you came across a harmless skeleton, you'd do well to take its advice. He is—or he used to be—one of us. You did meet him, right?

You help this guy out of the coffin and head back to 80.

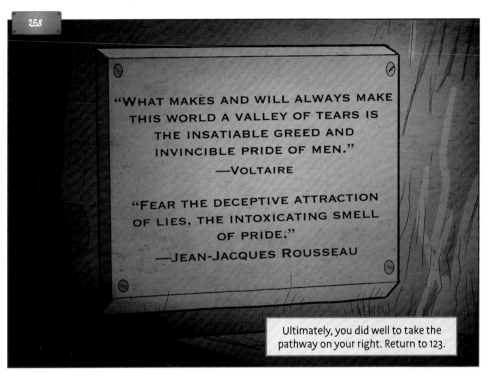

"WHAT MAKES AND WILL ALWAYS MAKE
THIS WORLD A VALLEY OF TEARS IS
THE INSATIABLE GREED AND
INVINCIBLE PRIDE OF MEN."
—VOLTAIRE

"FEAR THE DECEPTIVE ATTRACTION
OF LIES, THE INTOXICATING SMELL
OF PRIDE."
—JEAN-JACQUES ROUSSEAU

Ultimately, you did well to take the pathway on your right. Return to 123.

BLOOD DEMON
Magic 6

As soon as your droplets of blood fall into the center of the circle, a fiery shape appears! If you defeat it, you gain either 1 magic point or 1 technology point—your choice. Then proceed to 317.

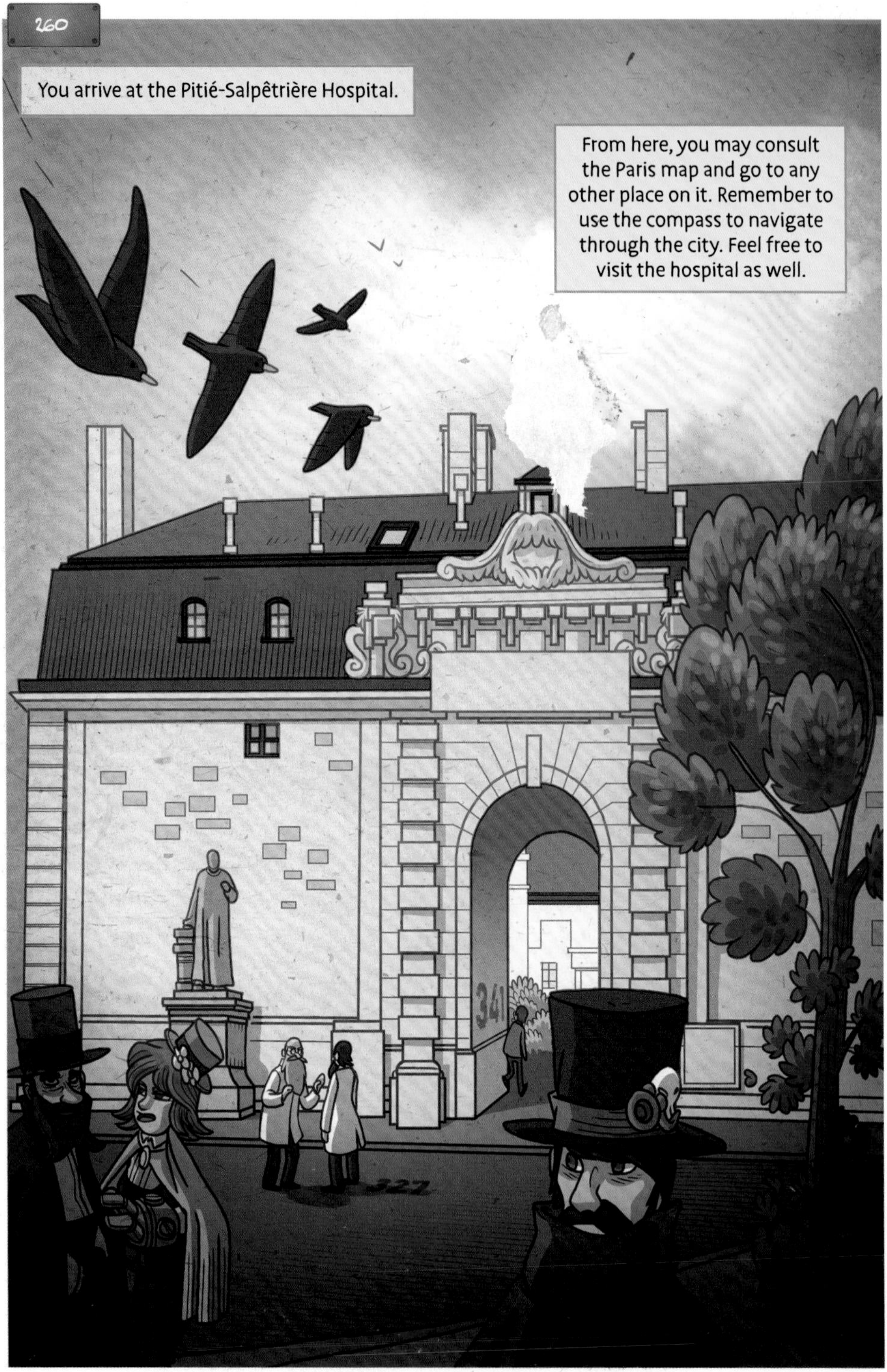
260
You arrive at the Pitié-Salpêtrière Hospital.
From here, you may consult the Paris map and go to any other place on it. Remember to use the compass to navigate through the city. Feel free to visit the hospital as well.
341
327

Welcome to my little book shop! You can call me Sophie. You look like a student. I think I have what you need on this shelf over here.

If you want to look at the shelf and perhaps purchase a book, head to 330. Otherwise, you can exit and return to 363.

It's time to take the plunge and complete the mission I hired you for: to fill the magic battery that powers the Eiffel Tower! Before you leave, here is a map of Paris and a compass. With these two items, you will be able to navigate to different places in the city where you are likely to find magic energy. I will explain how to use them.

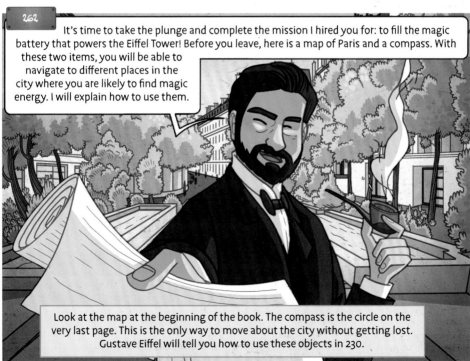

Look at the map at the beginning of the book. The compass is the circle on the very last page. This is the only way to move about the city without getting lost. Gustave Eiffel will tell you how to use these objects in 230.

PRIVATE

This door is locked. You're not able to pick the lock because a guard is watching you from the end of the hall. Return to 285.

264

Oh no, that's enough of your bootlicking! Get out of here!

You move away from the painting. It falls mute once again. Head to 244.

265

361

322

This hallway is blocked by an unknown force field. If you want to try to cross it, head to 391. If not, go back to 244.

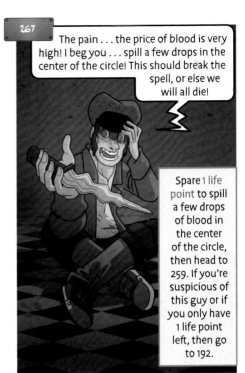

The pain . . . the price of blood is very high! I beg you . . . spill a few drops in the center of the circle! This should break the spell, or else we will all die!

Spare 1 life point to spill a few drops of blood in the center of the circle, then head to 259. If you're suspicious of this guy or if you only have 1 life point left, then go to 192.

Thank goodness! You seem like you come from a good family. You're in the School of Technomagic, aren't you? Then you must know Simon, my godson. He disappeared a few days ago in this museum.

Will you help us find him?

Since you discovered that factory secrets were being sold to a spy, the workers are thankful! Or at least some of them are. You're done with this place. You can now consult the Paris map and go to a different location with the help of your compass.

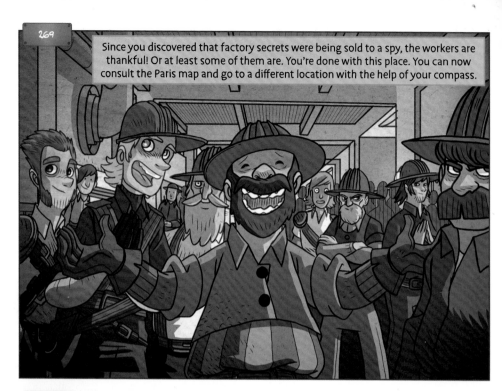

OF PRIDE."
—JEAN-JACQUES ROUSSEAU

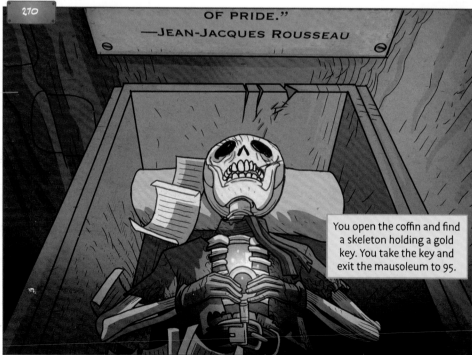

You open the coffin and find a skeleton holding a gold key. You take the key and exit the mausoleum to 95.

You don't seem . . . how should I say . . . as fine a person as our Simon. He is a technomagic student like you. Leave us. You are of no interest to us.

Such snobbery—and all because you don't have the right clothes. Return to 323.

186

You slowly awaken . . . but where are you? You've never seen this place before.

273

You ignore your professor and head straight for the cage. A big dog is looking at you. If you want to try to pet it, go to 251. Otherwise, head to 139.

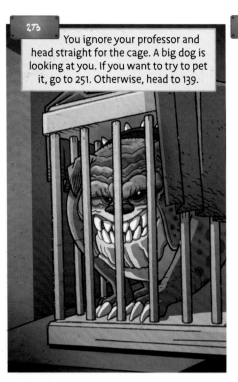

274

Mmmm, a nice hot coffee! This short break allows you to gain 1 life point if you have 2 or fewer lives. Check your map again and continue on to your chosen destination.

275

The answer is: hurricane. Yes, hurry and cane!

If you had the right answer, you gain 1 life point. Head back to talk to Doctor Charcot in 388.

276

Welcome to the weapons factory of the Boulogne Swamp. What can I do for you?

If your character is a girl, say that you want to take a tour of the factory and head to 343. If your character is a boy, pretend you are a worker in 393.

277

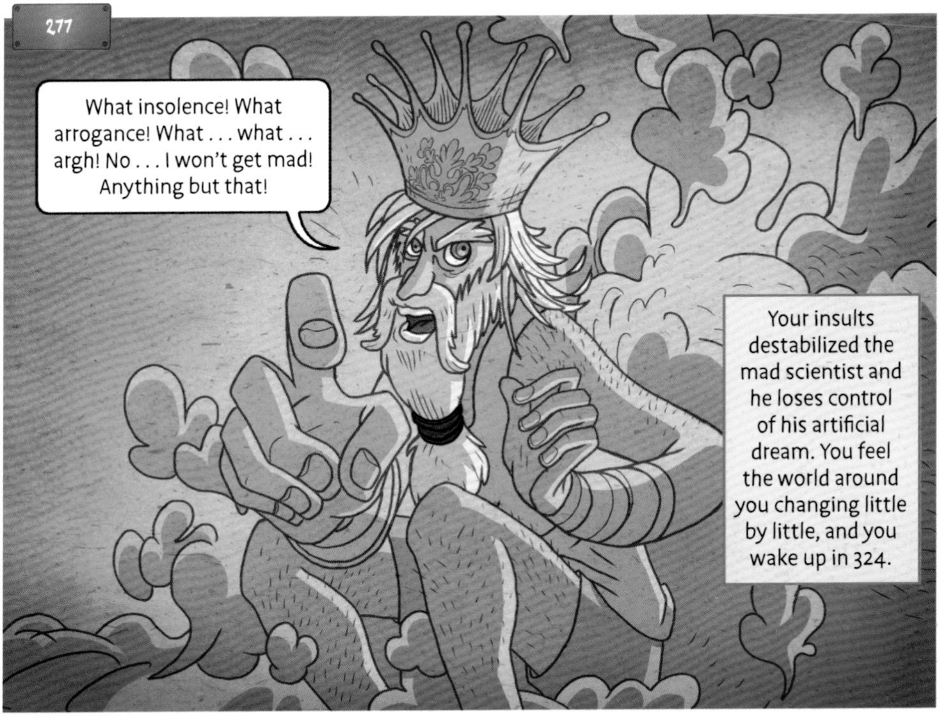
What insolence! What arrogance! What . . . what . . . argh! No . . . I won't get mad! Anything but that!
Your insults destabilized the mad scientist and he loses control of his artificial dream. You feel the world around you changing little by little, and you wake up in 324.

278

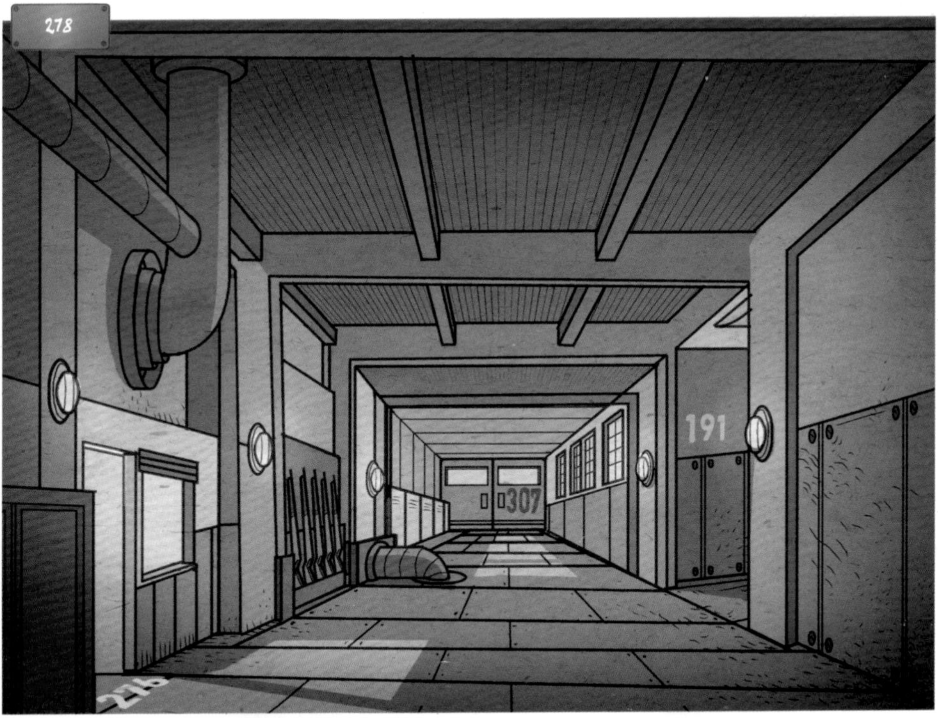
191
307
276

Cough! Cough! Whoever you are, thank you. Be careful—she must still be lurking around here somewhere! She'll get you, too, you know . . .

This rich guy was buried alive, but thankfully you walked by and saved him. If you want to take advantage of the situation and take his money, head to 129. If you want to ask who he's talking about, then go to 257.

Of course! Thanks to you, the opera is free of this dangerous chemist (although the audience seemed to enjoy his mischief). Please accept this statue. It was a gift to me from a wealthy patron. Goodbye, and thanks again!

The director gives you 50 francs and this strange artifact, which is a source of magic. It adds 5 energy points to your magic battery. You are finished at the Opera House. Consult your map of Paris and go to your next destination, with the help of your compass.

TECH ZOMBIE
Technology 5

A tech zombie is blocking the pathway! After you vanquish him, you may return the way you came in 9, or continue on in 333.

Stop right there! Authorized personnel only are allowed in this wing of the hospital.

If you don't have permission to pass, you must go back to 341. If you do have permission, head on to 352.

284

Your karma is influenced by your decisions. I am the lady who will judge them and write them down! What happened when you faced the king?

If you gave the ring to the painting of the king, the voice gives you 2 points. If you took his crown, the voice gives you 1 point. Remember your score and head to 301.

If you didn't visit the Louvre fully—looking at both paintings, analyzing a statue, and talking to a deranged student—then head back to 23.

285

286

You must have helped my patients if they let you in here. Well done! You're just in time. I have cured this woman and I need you for another experiment.

You are now a guinea pig for the doctor's project. Go to 320.

This bag was lost by a student or a professor, no doubt. Thanks for bringing it back without going through it. What a well-raised person you are! As thanks, here are 50 francs.

Your honesty paid off! Write that you got 50 francs in your inventory. Always remember to update those notes. Return to 223.

The crate holds a divination spell as well as a magic crystal! It add 5 energy points to your battery. Now go to the lobby of the factory in 269.

They are destroying everything in the name of progress! I beg you, please punish those who did this. Find a chest in the swamp and take the contents. What is inside will help you sabotage the factory's secret project.

Whatever you think of her request, you got a good scare and you lose 1 life point—unless your magic score is 6 or higher. Go back to 334.

Is it me, or did this painting just move? If you want to touch it, head to 335. Otherwise, go back to 244.

En garde!

If you lose this fight, you find yourself safe and sound in 403 with 1 life point remaining. If you win, head to 407.

ABDELATIF, ALGERIAN WIZARD
Magic 10
Technology 8

These people start asking you questions. If you're wearing a gentleman's outfit or a lady's outfit, go to 268. If not, go to 271.

You're hearing voices. To answer politely, head to 264. If you want to return this gentleman's insult, go to 313. To back away slowly, return to 244. If you choose the last option, you will be able to come back to this painting later.

294

Some members of high society are chatting before the show. If you want to talk to them, head to 195. Otherwise, return to 209.

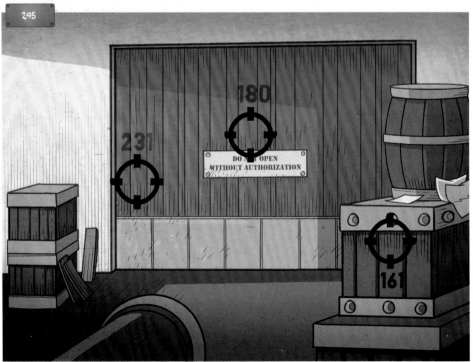

295

296

A ghost appears as you approach the ruins of the fountain. If you want to talk to her, head to 289. If you're worried that she's just another obstacle, quietly back up to 334.

297

In the nightstand, you find a strange figurine of a blind woman with a scale and a sword in her hands. Take it and return to 211.

298

349

176

306

Oh, yes . . . the famous ghost. Since it possessed the opera singer, our shows have been sold out every night for two weeks! If you're lucky, she'll let you see her before her performance. But you'll have to figure out the password first.

If you want to talk to the opera singer, you'll first have to figure out the password. Maybe someone else here can help you. Head back to 255.

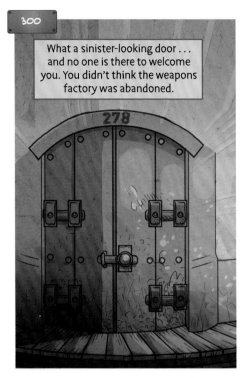

What a sinister-looking door . . . and no one is there to welcome you. You didn't think the weapons factory was abandoned.

You stole the ring to feed his royal greed, or faced up to his tantrum and took the crown from his head. What did you do when you faced the knight?

If you took the painting of the knight, the voice rewards you with 3 points. If you didn't take it, you receive 1 point. Add this result to your previous one, remember it, and head to 254.

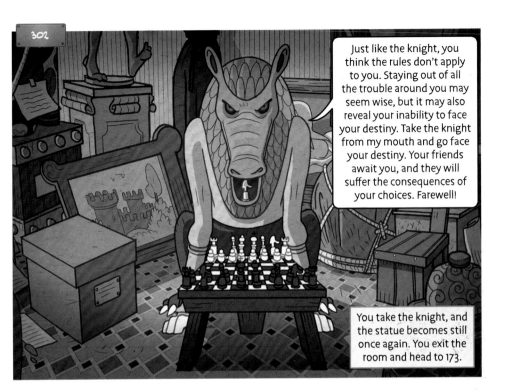

Just like the knight, you think the rules don't apply to you. Staying out of all the trouble around you may seem wise, but it may also reveal your inability to face your destiny. Take the knight from my mouth and go face your destiny. Your friends await you, and they will suffer the consequences of your choices. Farewell!

You take the knight, and the statue becomes still once again. You exit the room and head to 173.

We're so close to meeting the greatest opera singer of our time, but we can't figure out the last part of her riddle! Here's the clue: I am a four-letter word that means sagacious, perspicacious, and sapient. The problem is, we don't know what any of those words mean!

This sounds like the last part of a three-part riddle. The answer will be the password you need to enter the singer's dressing room. Return to 255.

304

If you have enough money to pay for a ticket, or if you already have a ticket, then head to 238. Otherwise, return to 209.

TICKETS

150 FRANCS

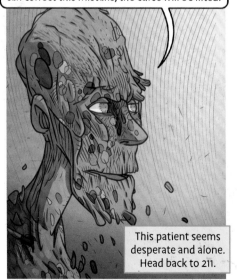

305

I am the leper, lonely and skeletal. The blind Lady Justice is given to me, but what I am looking for will cut away my suffering. If you can correct this mistake, the curse will be lifted.

This patient seems desperate and alone. Head back to 211.

306

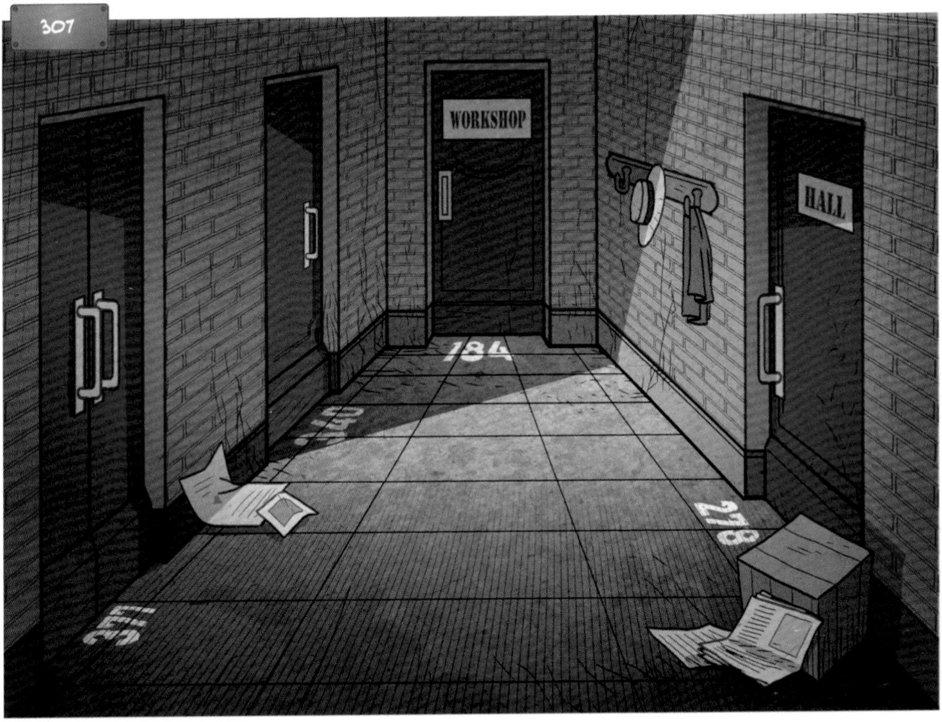
307
WORKSHOP
HALL
184
278
233

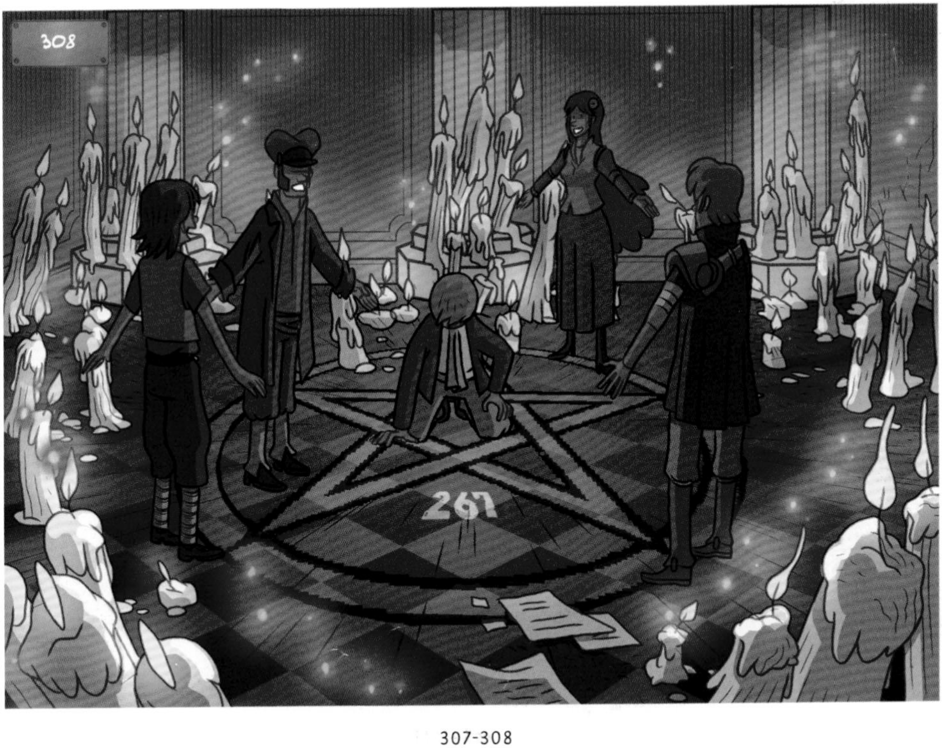
308
267

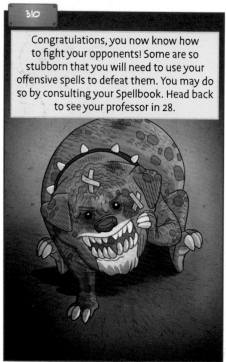

Congratulations, you now know how to fight your opponents! Some are so stubborn that you will need to use your offensive spells to defeat them. You may do so by consulting your Spellbook. Head back to see your professor in 28.

You climb down the ladder and find yourself in a damp underground passageway. You take the torch on the wall and start walking.

312

Click . . . click . . . and the door opens! You were able to pick the lock successfully. Enter the house quickly in 385.

313

It's nice to hear something other than the bland conversation of sophisticated museum visitors for a change. I like your straight talk!

It this a hallucination? The painting is talking to you! You can continue the conversation in 397, but should you? If you decide not to, return to 244. You will not be able to come back to this painting.

314

What a surprise! I was expecting someone older, but you're around my age. What can I do for you?

You can ask her about the famous ghost in 204, or request her help to get you backstage in 249.

315

The opera singer is as clever as she is talented! We couldn't even figure out the first part of her riddle: I am a two-syllable word with several meanings. I am long and flat, I am good with numbers, and I often disagree.

This sounds like the beginning of a three-part riddle. The answer will be the password that you need to enter the singer's dressing room. Return to 255.

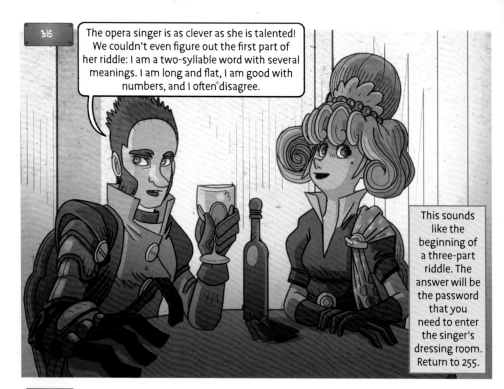

316

You have a magic score and a technology score, just like your opponents. First, decide which one of these scores you will use in combat. Then look at the Wheel of Destiny at the back of the book. You can spin a crayon or toss a small object like a coin, taking note of the number it lands on or closest to. (You may also use a die instead of the wheel.) Write down the number you get, then add it to your magic or technology score—whichever you wish. This is your combat score. Do this once for yourself and once for your opponent. You and your opponent must fight with the same skill—either magic or technology. If the result is in your favor, you defeat your opponent. If the result is in your opponent's favor, you lose 1 life point and have to fight again. If you tie, you must fight until one of you wins.

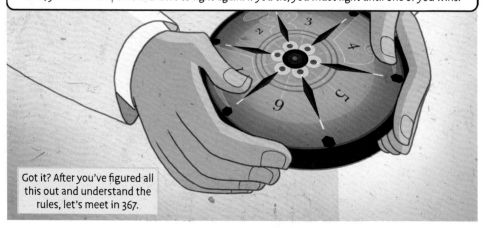

Got it? After you've figured all this out and understand the rules, let's meet in 367.

No, no! The demon was talking through me... What did you do? Simon is hurt. But... but the spell is broken!

This is what Ammit's statue was talking about. You acted with good intentions, but there was still a tragic consequence: The student Simon was hurt. You leave to find help in 399.

Congratulations! During the singer's performance, we saw you stumble onto the stage like a puppet... then we heard a scream backstage, and at that moment everybody woke up. The air smelled foul of gas. Then you tripped against the stage props and fainted. While you were unconscious, we found out where the scream came from. There was a mad scientist in the basement! He's the one behind all of this.

So that's that. If you want to ask the director for a reward, head to 280. If you're feeling altruistic and don't want a reward, go to 387.

You're going to have to use your technomage powers against the ancient powers of my Algerian coworker. They have a very different approach to magic. Prepare yourself—here is Abdelatif!

It seems like you're going to have to duel this guy. Get ready and head to 291.

Well, that was a close one. You search his belongings and find 50 francs. Shake it off and continue in 37.

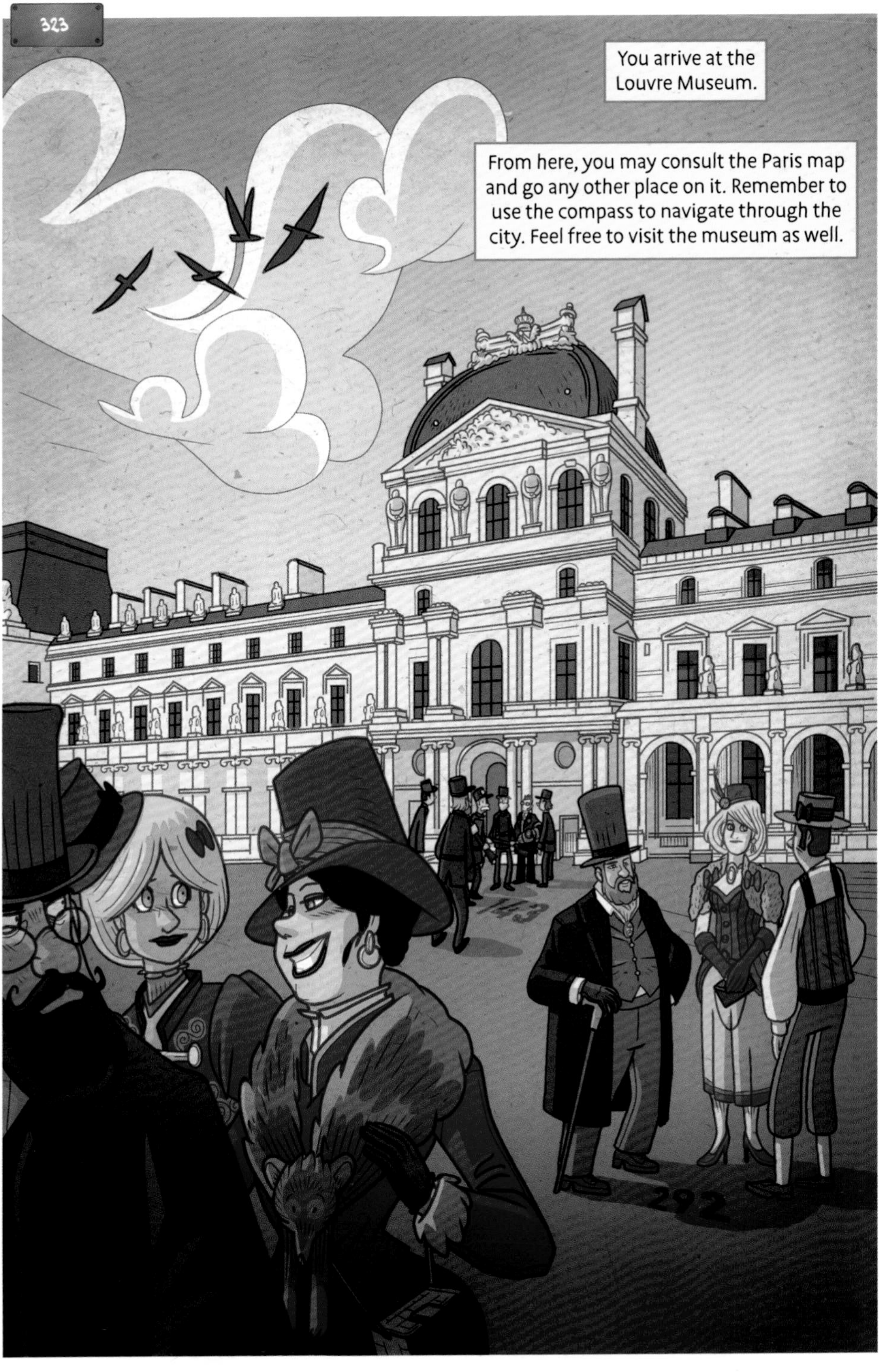
323
You arrive at the Louvre Museum.
From here, you may consult the Paris map and go any other place on it. Remember to use the compass to navigate through the city. Feel free to visit the museum as well.
143
292

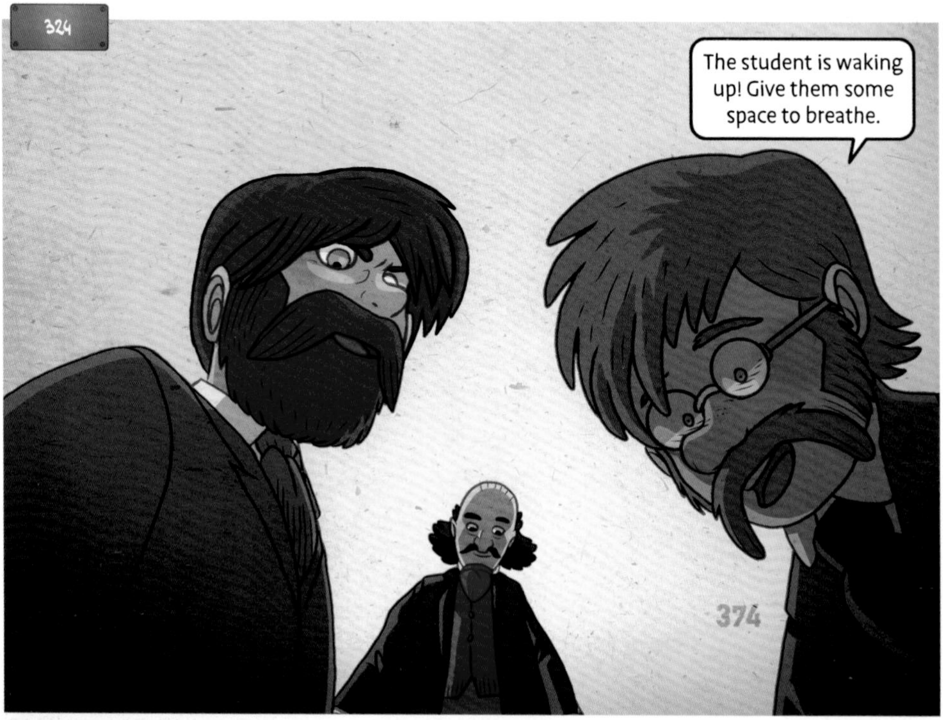
324
The student is waking up! Give them some space to breathe.
374

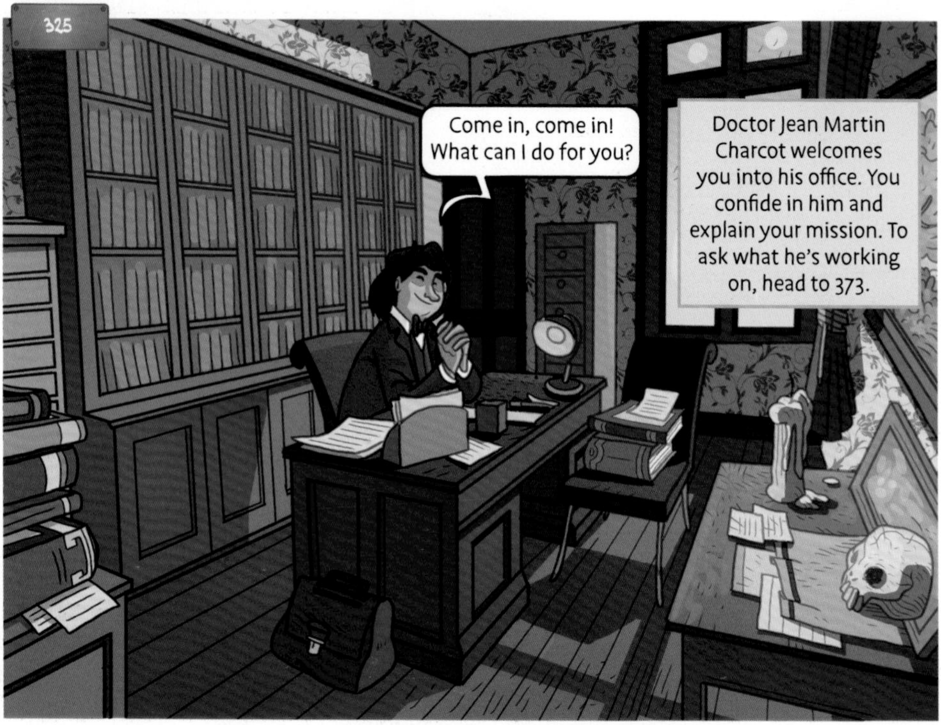
325
Come in, come in! What can I do for you?
Doctor Jean Martin Charcot welcomes you into his office. You confide in him and explain your mission. To ask what he's working on, head to 373.

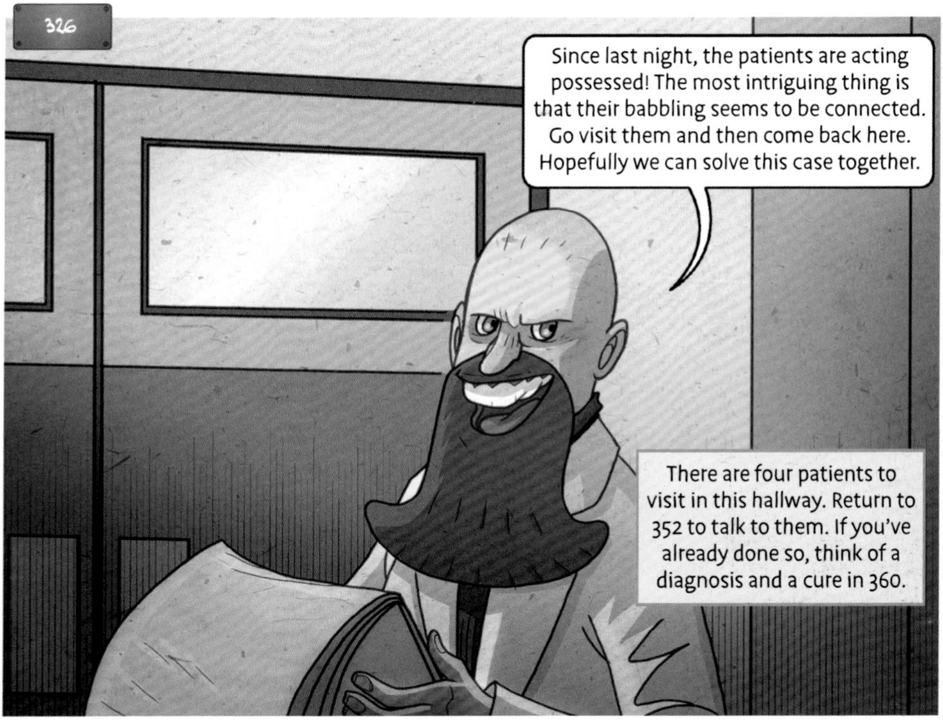
326
Since last night, the patients are acting possessed! The most intriguing thing is that their babbling seems to be connected. Go visit them and then come back here. Hopefully we can solve this case together.
There are four patients to visit in this hallway. Return to 352 to talk to them. If you've already done so, think of a diagnosis and a cure in 360.

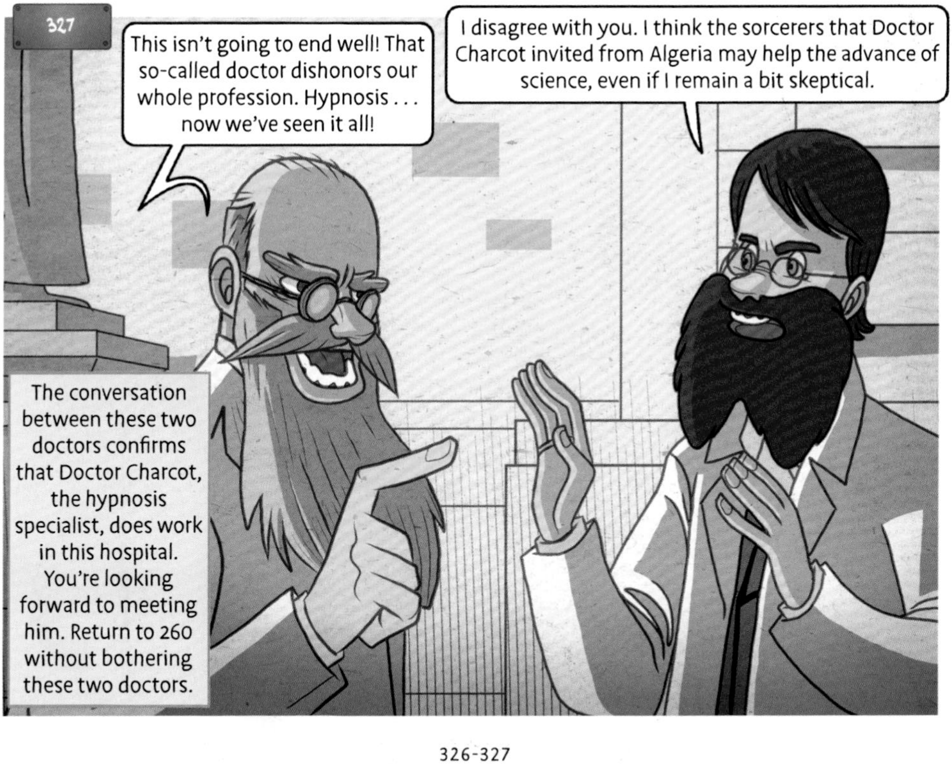
327
This isn't going to end well! That so-called doctor dishonors our whole profession. Hypnosis . . . now we've seen it all!
I disagree with you. I think the sorcerers that Doctor Charcot invited from Algeria may help the advance of science, even if I remain a bit skeptical.
The conversation between these two doctors confirms that Doctor Charcot, the hypnosis specialist, does work in this hospital. You're looking forward to meeting him. Return to 260 without bothering these two doctors.

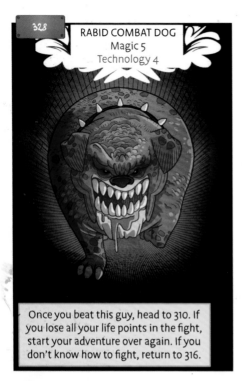

328

RABID COMBAT DOG
Magic 5
Technology 4

Once you beat this guy, head to 310. If you lose all your life points in the fight, start your adventure over again. If you don't know how to fight, return to 316.

329

345   163

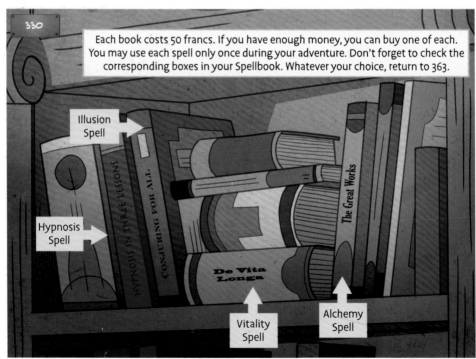

330

Each book costs 50 francs. If you have enough money, you can buy one of each. You may use each spell only once during your adventure. Don't forget to check the corresponding boxes in your Spellbook. Whatever your choice, return to 363.

Illusion Spell

Hypnosis Spell

Vitality Spell

Alchemy Spell

331

I beg you to save my Simon! He's so fragile . . . Here, take this pass. If you show it to the guards, they will let you through. Please find my sweet little duckling!

You have the documents you need to enter the museum. Head back to 323.

332

DRESSING ROOM

So, what's the password? You only have one chance to get it right!

If you found the word "counterclockwise," then you may enter and meet the singer in 314. If you didn't know it or got it wrong, return to 112. You cannot try to see her again.

333

300

334

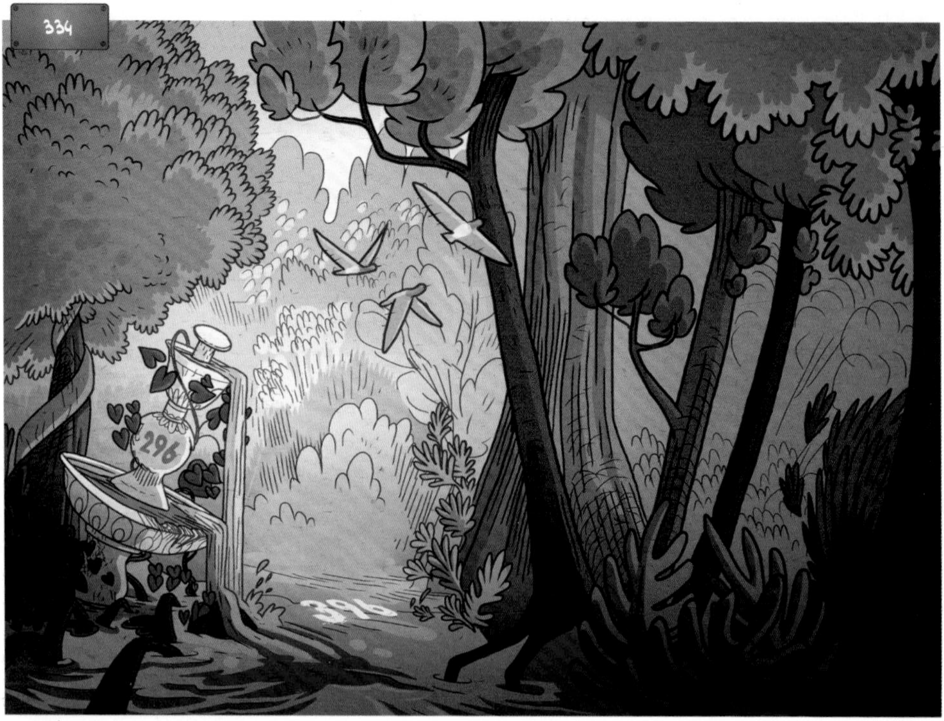
296
396

335

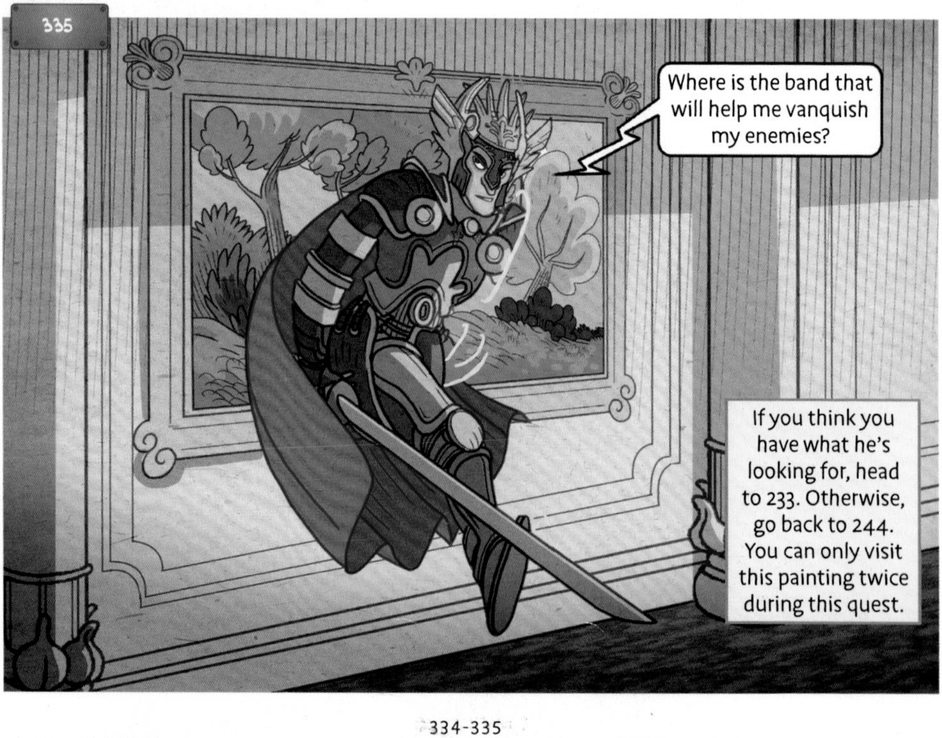
Where is the band that will help me vanquish my enemies?
If you think you have what he's looking for, head to 233. Otherwise, go back to 244. You can only visit this painting twice during this quest.

336

During your travels, a woman stops you and offers to sell you a spell scroll. Once you've finished with her, check your map and proceed to the destination you chose.

Hello, young technomage. You can buy any spell you want for 150 francs.

337

This is for you, from Doctor Charcot. Thank you for all your help!

This magic crystal adds 6 energy points to your battery. You're done with this place, so travel to another location with the help of your compass.

338

Did you really think that was going to work? Plus it seems to have alerted the neighborhod to your location. You feel a presence behind you. You turn around and find yourself face to face with . . . well, go see in 166.

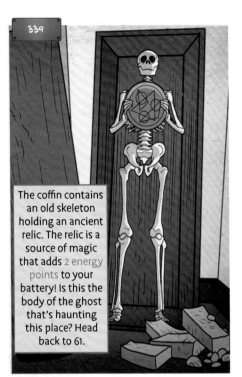

339

The coffin contains an old skeleton holding an ancient relic. The relic is a source of magic that adds 2 energy points to your battery! Is this the body of the ghost that's haunting this place? Head back to 61.

340

This door is blocked. Head back to 307.

341

You interrupted us at the very moment the demon was finally going to accept our sacrifice! Curse you!

They don't seem very friendly. To teach them a lesson, head to 379. To try to calm them down, go to 252.

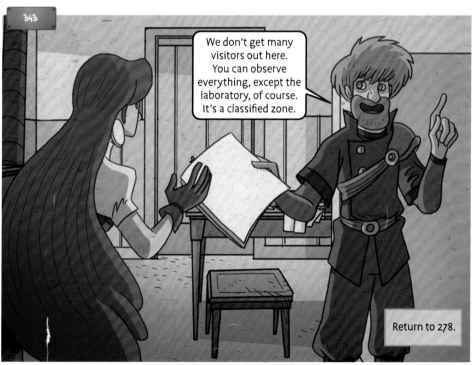

We don't get many visitors out here. You can observe everything, except the laboratory, of course. It's a classified zone.

Return to 278.

You search the bag and find a small healing potion that will give you 1 life point whenever you need it. You can use it only once. Now head back to 223.

Your presence has angered these rats. They try to bite you!

RATS
Magic 5
Technology 3

If you win the fight against the vermin, continue to 232.

Farewell.

You give the ring to the king. And that's it! Return to 244. You will not be able to look at this painting again.

What an interesting duel that was! I have to admit, that wasn't the outcome I expected. Let's test the strength of your mind now, shall we? You will face Doress the Seer.

Continue the experiment in 185.

Nothing interesting happens while you travel through the city. Look at your map and continue on to your chosen destination.

Very well. Here's what you can do: Calm the patients of my unit; they seem anxious today. We can meet in my lab once you are finished. Take this—it will be useful to you.

You now have access to Doctor Charcot's unit. He also gives you a hypnosis spell. Head back to 341. You will not be able to come back here.

The coffin contains an old skeleton holding an energy blaster. The blaster adds 1 technology point to your score while you are at the Opera House. Don't forget, you can carry only one weapon at a time. Is this the body of the ghost that's haunting this place? Head back to 61.

You head back to the School of Technomagic.

There's nothing more to do here. Look at your Paris map and head to another destination. Remember to use the compass to navigate through the city.

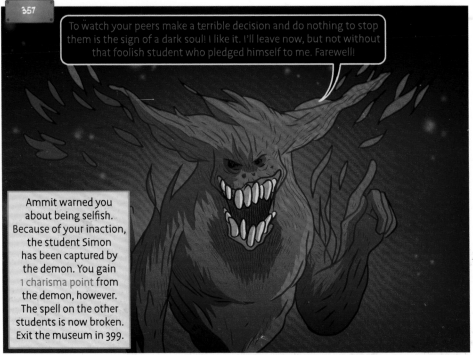

To watch your peers make a terrible decision and do nothing to stop them is the sign of a dark soul! I like it. I'll leave now, but not without that foolish student who pledged himself to me. Farewell!

Ammit warned you about being selfish. Because of your inaction, the student Simon has been captured by the demon. You gain 1 charisma point from the demon, however. The spell on the other students is now broken. Exit the museum in 399.

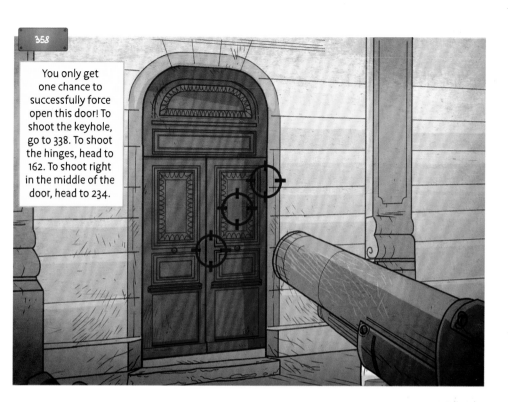

You only get one chance to successfully force open this door! To shoot the keyhole, go to 338. To shoot the hinges, head to 162. To shoot right in the middle of the door, head to 234.

That's all taken care of! The dead will no longer wander the world of the living because of this woman. I owe you big time. Here's a crystal I found while digging a grave last year. I hear they are precious!

The cemetery's gravedigger gives you a gift: a magic crystal that adds 5 energy points to your battery. You are finished here. You may consult your Paris map and head to another location, with the help of your compass.

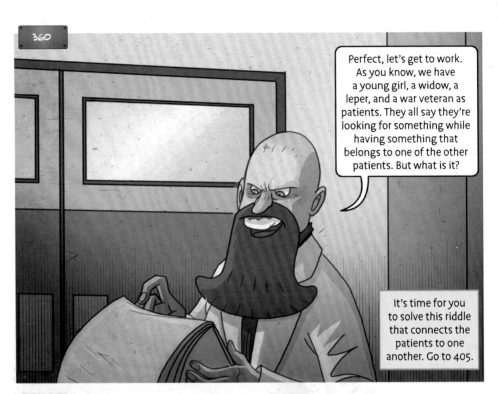

360

Perfect, let's get to work. As you know, we have a young girl, a widow, a leper, and a war veteran as patients. They all say they're looking for something while having something that belongs to one of the other patients. But what is it?

It's time for you to solve this riddle that connects the patients to one another. Go to 405.

361

In this old abandoned chest you find a copper tube. What can it be used for? Take it and continue in 322.

362

This is a demonic ritual. To interrupt it, head to 342. If you want to watch it unfold, continue in 357.

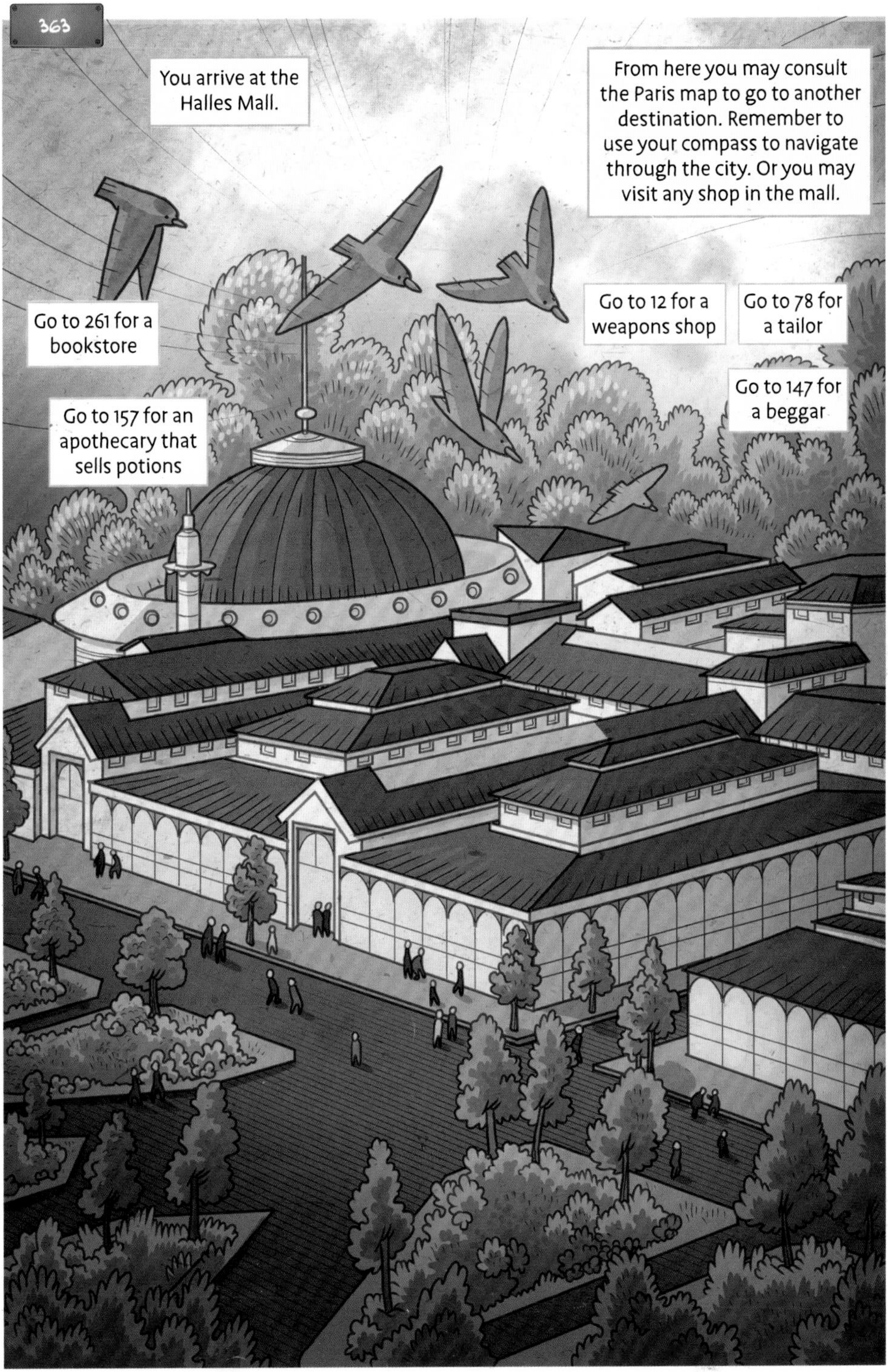
363
You arrive at the Halles Mall.
From here you may consult the Paris map to go to another destination. Remember to use your compass to navigate through the city. Or you may visit any shop in the mall.
Go to 261 for a bookstore
Go to 157 for an apothecary that sells potions
Go to 12 for a weapons shop
Go to 78 for a tailor
Go to 147 for a beggar

Traitor! That is not what I asked for!

KING
Magic 7
Technology 6

The painting is attacking you! If you neutralize it, you take its crown and head back to 244. You will not be able to look at this painting again.

Welcome to the Pitié-Salpêtrière Hospital! I'm sorry, but visitors are not allowed any farther. However, if you haven't met him yet, Doctor Charcot will see you now.

Return to 341.

Very well! I'm going to inject you with a substance that will increase your technology skills. Be warned—it's very painful.

Your technology score increases by 1 point, but at the cost of 2 life points. If this would kill you, or if you don't want to do it, refuse the shot. Exit the lab in 184. You won't be able to come back here.

Take a deep breath and face the mastiff in 328.

What a bright mind! Let's see just how bright ... Do you see that kennel over there? It holds a combat dog. If you can neutralize him, come back and see me. You won't need to use a spell for this encounter, even if you have one. You don't have a choice. Practice makes perfect, right?

LITTLE RED RIDING HOOD
Magic 4

243

218

Little Red Riding Hood wants to give you a black eye! If you've already come this way, you'll have to fight her again.

You walk down the backstage platform and tiptoe quietly toward the stage. The opera singer begins to sing. At that moment, you notice a pink vapor, and then . . .

That's exactly what you thought: There's a secret trapdoor under the boxes. Well done! If you want to go through it, head to 311. Otherwise, go back to 385.

This cannon is unattended. If you want to use it, you need to have 4 or more technology points; go to 295. But proceed at your own risk! Otherwise, return to 237.

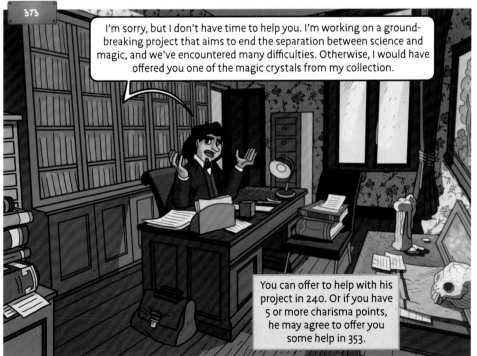

I'm sorry, but I don't have time to help you. I'm working on a ground-breaking project that aims to end the separation between science and magic, and we've encountered many difficulties. Otherwise, I would have offered you one of the magic crystals from my collection.

You can offer to help with his project in 240. Or if you have 5 or more charisma points, he may agree to offer you some help in 353.

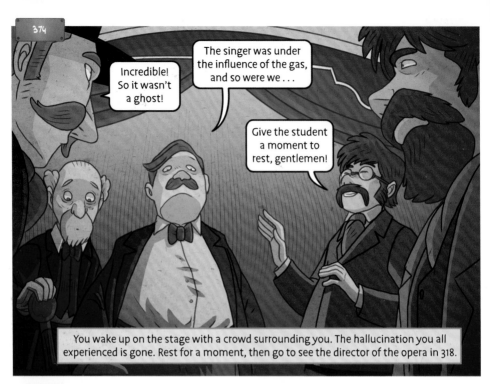

Incredible! So it wasn't a ghost!

The singer was under the influence of the gas, and so were we . . .

Give the student a moment to rest, gentlemen!

You wake up on the stage with a crowd surrounding you. The hallucination you all experienced is gone. Rest for a moment, then go to see the director of the opera in 318.

The scientists at the factory are playing with witchcraft. You exit this room immediately and return to 307.

February 15, 1889

The mechanical dogs are operational, but they have limitations. We need to find a way to blend flesh with steel. The lab is currently working on this breakthrough, but the government might forbid our experiments if we are discovered

MECHANICAL COMBAT DOG
Technology 5

Once you have pacified this creature, search the scattered documents on the ground in 375.

Once you search the desk, return to 385.

EVIL EYE SPELL

Neutralize them, then go to 392.

The sliding door is closed. It's impossible to open it, except with the use of tremendous firepower, which is likely to get you in trouble. Return to 237.

DO NOT OPEN
WITHOUT AUTHORIZATION

383

You find a green potion. You drink it and it gives you 1 life point, but only if you have 3 or fewer life points. Otherwise, it has no effect. Return to 306.

384

I don't know what's behind that door at the end of the warehouse. None of the workers have access to it. Sometimes I see the director go through it at night. He's hiding something from us, I just know it!

This piece of information heightens your curiosity. You return to 237.

385

This old house is a mess. It looks like it was broken into recently, which is odd because the door was locked from the inside.

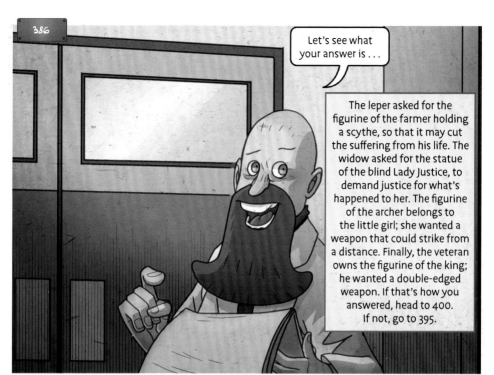

Let's see what your answer is . . .

The leper asked for the figurine of the farmer holding a scythe, so that it may cut the suffering from his life. The widow asked for the statue of the blind Lady Justice, to demand justice for what's happened to her. The figurine of the archer belongs to the little girl; she wanted a weapon that could strike from a distance. Finally, the veteran owns the figurine of the king; he wanted a double-edged weapon. If that's how you answered, head to 400. If not, go to 395.

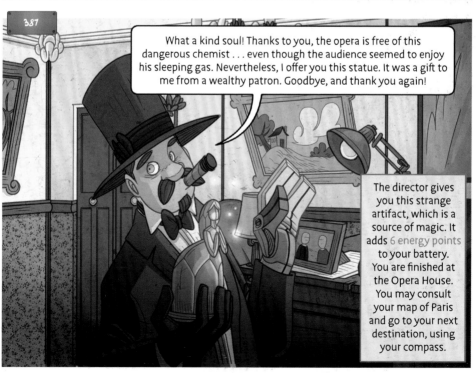

What a kind soul! Thanks to you, the opera is free of this dangerous chemist . . . even though the audience seemed to enjoy his sleeping gas. Nevertheless, I offer you this statue. It was a gift to me from a wealthy patron. Goodbye, and thank you again!

The director gives you this strange artifact, which is a source of magic. It adds 6 energy points to your battery. You are finished at the Opera House. You may consult your map of Paris and go to your next destination, using your compass.

Thank you, you've been such a great help! I bet that once the mission is over, we'll find a way to work together. I'll continue now with our Algerian friends; they were really impressed by your mind and your magic. As a thank-you, I want to offer you part of my magic crystal collection. Ask the front desk for it. Goodbye!

You're done with Doctor Charcot's experiments. You exit the room and go to the hospital lobby in 337.

Nothing much happens on your journey, except that you meet this adorable puppy! Look at your map and continue on to the destination of your choice.

The patients are behaving strangely today. They're all talking about something they have but don't want, and something they want but don't have. Ask the on-call doctor. He knows more than I do.

Return to 352.

391

All that is left of you after your attempt is a pile of ash. Start your adventure over again.

392

You saved my life, and I owe you! I think this fight broke the spell that we were under.

Ammit found cynicism and greed in your soul, but you have listened to her advice. You saved the group of students, including Simon, who offers you a copy of a spell of your choice in thanks. Leave the museum in 399.

393

New to the team, huh? I hope you're a healthy one! Remember that you may not enter the lab. Only the scientists have access.

Return to 278.

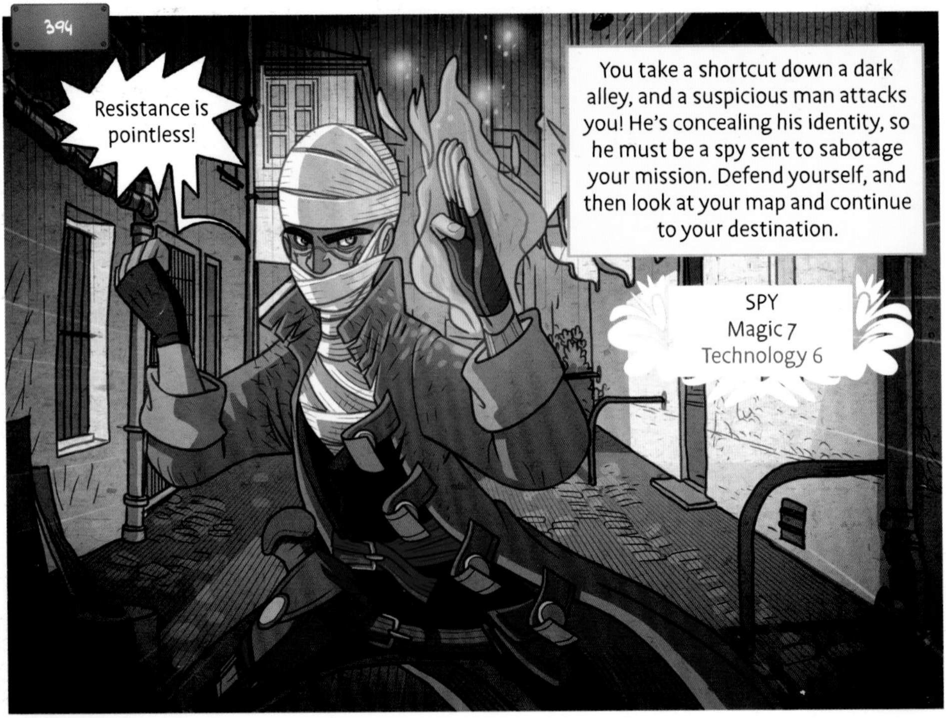
394
Resistance is pointless!
You take a shortcut down a dark alley, and a suspicious man attacks you! He's concealing his identity, so he must be a spy sent to sabotage your mission. Defend yourself, and then look at your map and continue to your destination.
SPY
Magic 7
Technology 6

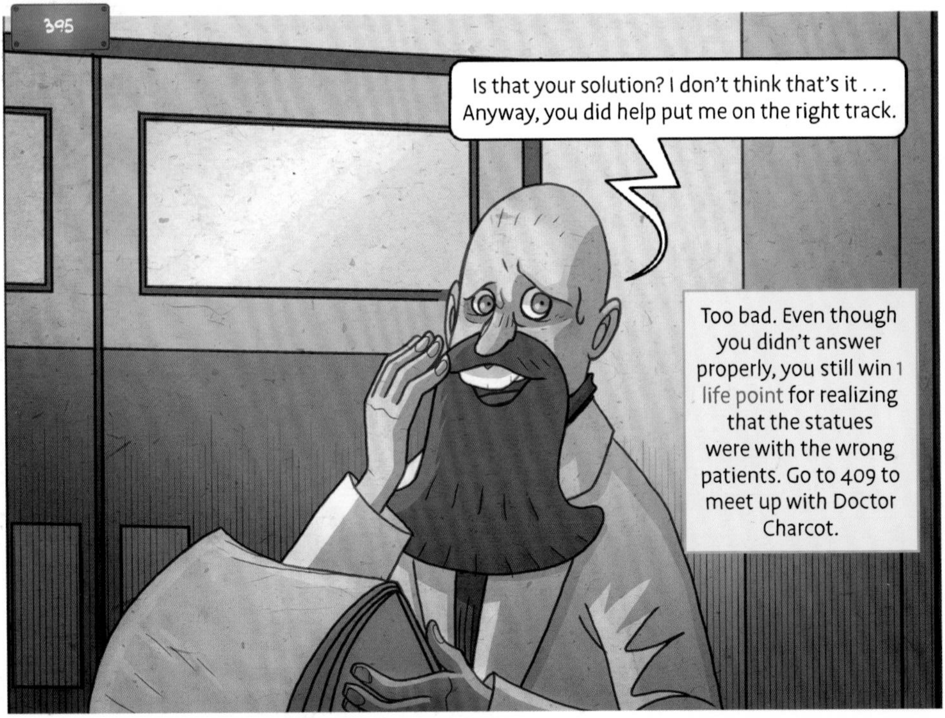
395
Is that your solution? I don't think that's it . . . Anyway, you did help put me on the right track.
Too bad. Even though you didn't answer properly, you still win 1 life point for realizing that the statues were with the wrong patients. Go to 409 to meet up with Doctor Charcot.

I've been stuck in this painting for over a century. You look adventurous, like me. Please set me free!

Help him with his request in 402, or return to 244 if you've heard enough. If you choose to leave, the painting won't talk to you anymore.

You arrive on a balcony overlooking the stage. The opera singer is about to make her entrance. You need to be as close as possible to observe her. Head backstage in 401.

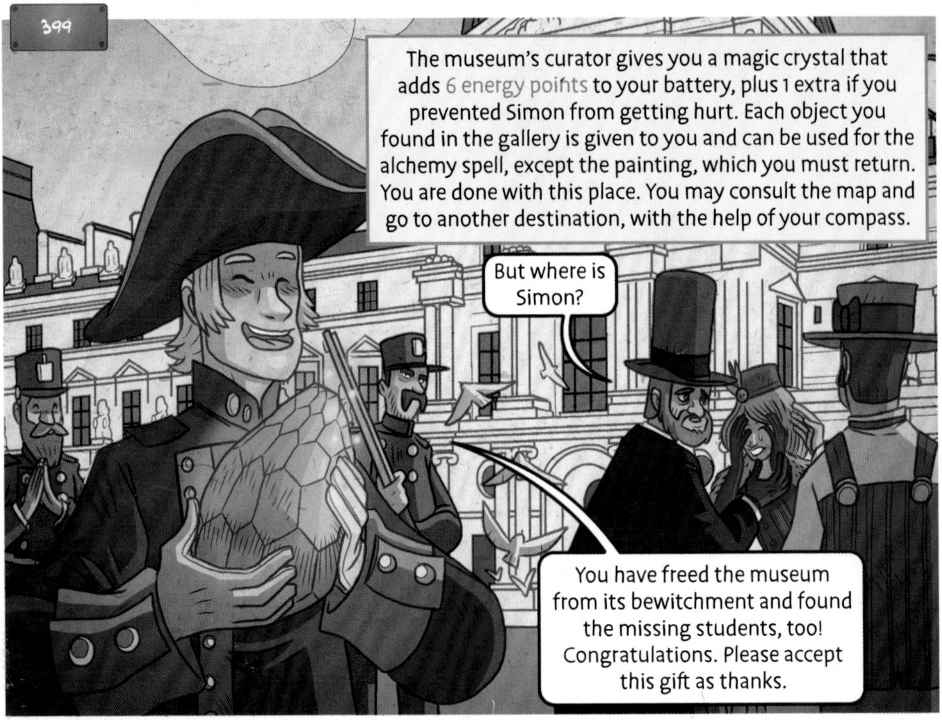
399
The museum's curator gives you a magic crystal that adds 6 energy points to your battery, plus 1 extra if you prevented Simon from getting hurt. Each object you found in the gallery is given to you and can be used for the alchemy spell, except the painting, which you must return. You are done with this place. You may consult the map and go to another destination, with the help of your compass.
But where is Simon?
You have freed the museum from its bewitchment and found the missing students, too! Congratulations. Please accept this gift as thanks.

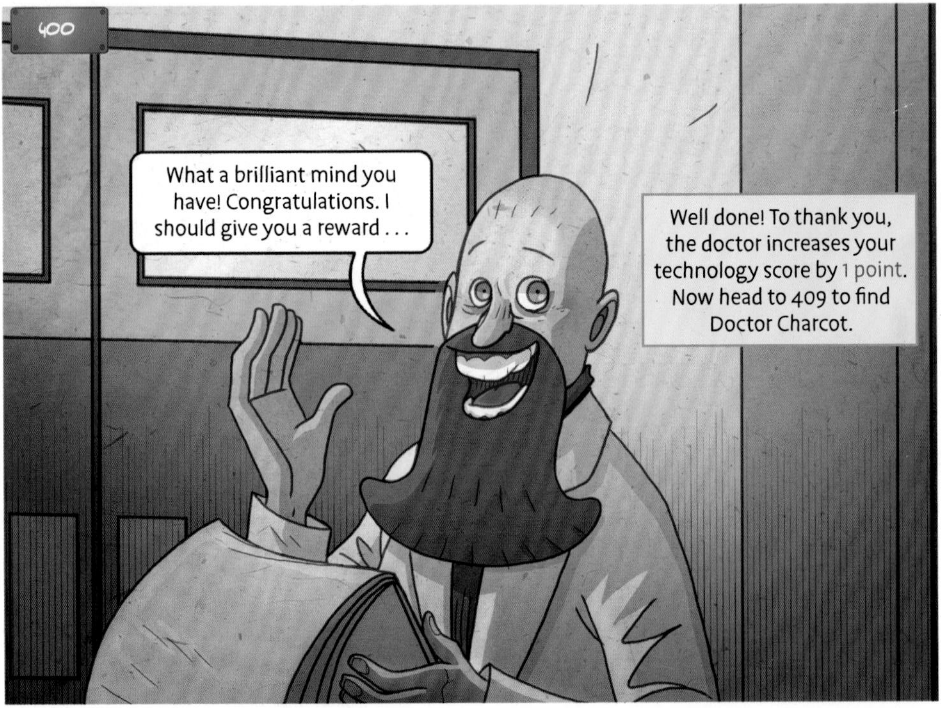
400
What a brilliant mind you have! Congratulations. I should give you a reward . . .
Well done! To thank you, the doctor increases your technology score by 1 point. Now head to 409 to find Doctor Charcot.

You take the painting of the knight off the wall, roll up the canvas, and put it in your bag. Was this a good idea? Return to 244.

Promising, but insufficient. Your magic is very strange . . .

You couldn't beat this wizard. Go see Doctor Charcot in 350.

Wise. You went straight for what you wanted instead of thinking about it, or else you showed restraint. Finally, how did you react when you faced the madman?

If you tried to comfort the student, the voice rewards your action with 1 point. If you pointed out his foolishness instead, she rewards your action with 3 points. Add your points to your three previous scores, remember your number, and head to 121.

Well done! You noticed that there is a small figurine in each of the bedrooms, but none of them are with their rightful owners. Each patient gave a clue about which figurine belongs to them. The figurines may be able to heal them.

Let's meet in 386. Remember which figurine you think belongs to each patient.

Sniff . . . my beautiful Lucette! She is gone . . . Is she with someone else? Oh! Who goes there? En garde!

He thinks you're an enemy! If you want to fight him, head to 111. If you want to try to talk to him, head to 34.

You are very impressive, young technomagician. You have earned my respect, and you deserve a reward.

Congratulations! Abdelatif gives you 50 francs and a copy of the Evil Eye Spell. Go see Doctor Charcot in 350.

ROBBER
Magic 5
Technology 4

You're passing through this park when a robber jumps out of the bushes and attacks you! Neutralize him, then look at your map and continue on to your chosen destination.

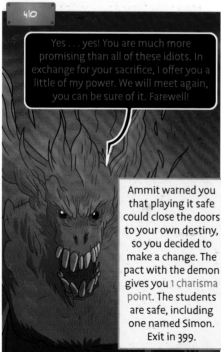

Yes . . . yes! You are much more promising than all of these idiots. In exchange for your sacrifice, I offer you a little of my power. We will meet again, you can be sure of it. Farewell!

Ammit warned you that playing it safe could close the doors to your own destiny, so you decided to make a change. The pact with the demon gives you 1 charisma point. The students are safe, including one named Simon. Exit in 399.

The crate holds an illusion spell as well as a magic crystal! It adds 5 energy points to your battery. Now go to the lobby of the factory in 269.

x

Halt, technomage! You may not enter unless you have completed your mission.

You arrive at the Champ de Mars to finish your quest. But have you completely filled your magic battery? If you're not sure, check your inventory. If it isn't full, choose another destination on your map and continue your journey. If the battery is full, you may continue to 413.

Oh, Mr. Eiffel will be very pleased! Hurry, he is waiting for you at the ceremony site. You'll find him at the foot of his tower.

I knew I could count on you! You can be proud of what you've accomplished. I know it was a difficult and dangerous mission, and no one besides me would have bet that a student could save this project!

The gatekeeper allows you to enter the World's Fair. Don't waste any time—go directly to 414.

You give your full magic battery to Gustave Eiffel and go with him to 415.

The steel tower, now filled with energy crystals, begins to vibrate and crackle with powerful magic. The crowd is enthralled by this unique and enchanting spectacle . . .

Yet no one seems to realize that the world has just entered a new era in the art of war. Nevertheless, you don't want to ruin the moment with such grim thoughts. For now, everything is fine, and the country is at peace.

Yes, for now, all is well.

THE END.

WHEEL OF DESTINY

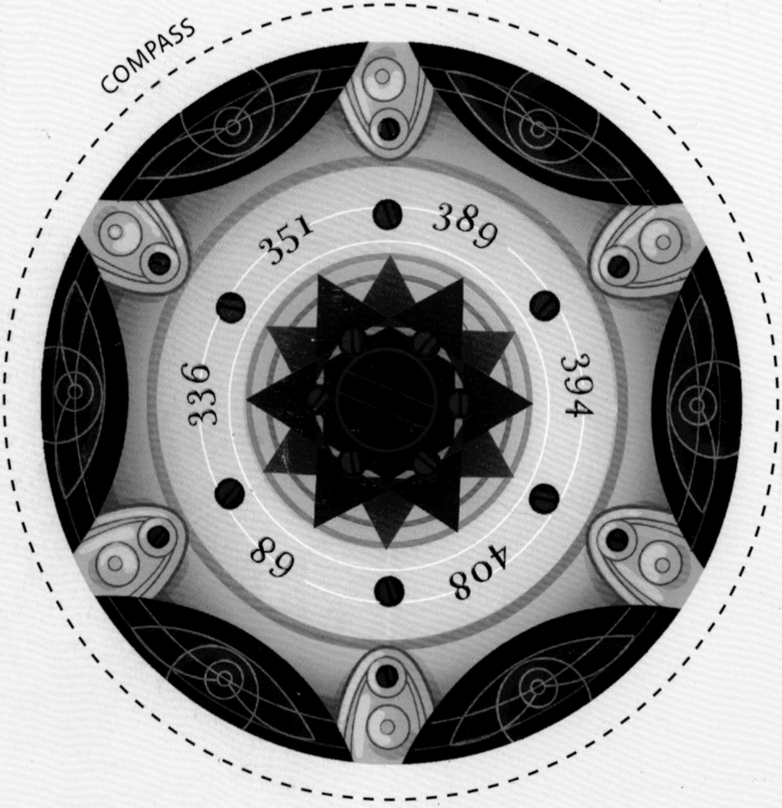
COMPASS
389
394
408
68
336
351